THE CASE AT BARTON MANOR

Mrs. Lillywhite Investigates
BOOK ONE

EMILY QUEEN

The Case at Barton Manor

ISBN- 978-1094741567

First Edition

Printed in the U.S.A.

Table of Contents

Chapter One 1

Chapter Two.. 8

Chapter Three 13

Chapter Four... 18

Chapter Five 22

Chapter Six.. 28

Chapter Seven 35

Chapter Eight.. 40

Chapter Nine 45

Chapter Ten... 49

Chapter Eleven 54

Chapter Twelve 60

Chapter Thirteen... 65

Chapter Fourteen 71

Chapter Fifteen.. 74

Chapter Sixteen 80

Chapter Seventeen... 85

Chapter Eighteen 89

Chapter Nineteen.. 94

Chapter Twenty 100

Chapter Twenty-One 104

Chapter Twenty-Two 108

Chapter Twenty-Three 113

Chapter Twenty-Four 118

Chapter Twenty-Five..124

Chapter Twenty-Six 128

Chapter Twenty-Seven 132

Chapter Twenty-Eight..138

Chapter Twenty-Nine 144

Chapter Thirty 150

CHAPTER ONE

Rosemary brushed a lock of honey-colored hair out of her eyes and pushed on the corner of the desk with all her might, letting out a harrumph when it refused to budge even an inch.

"Wadsworth!" she called, straightening the bodice of her dress while soft footsteps descended the stairs. By the time the butler entered the room, she'd set herself back to rights—or, at least, what accounted for rights to Rosemary. According to her mother, she'd become far too familiar with her staff.

"Madam?" Wadsworth bowed slightly towards his mistress, his expression unwavering, but with an effort. "Are you in need of assistance?"

Rosemary glanced back at the desk and then again at Wadsworth, suddenly uncertain whether the task was beyond a man of his years. "I'll need a crate for Andrew's things, and then we'll discuss the furniture."

"Yes, of course, madam. Right away." He appeared to have an opinion on the subject but wisely kept his thoughts to himself as he strode back out the door, closing it softly behind him. He needn't have commented anyway, because his expression indicated the direction his thoughts had taken.

Maybe Wadsworth is right, Rosemary thought. After all, it had been less than a year since her husband, Andrew Lillywhite, had passed away, and the shock had yet to dissipate. Each time Rosemary left the townhouse, she was forced to walk past the sign out the front reading Lillywhite Investigations, and each time it was a knife to the heart. The ground-floor office would be better used as an art studio and would carry far fewer memories of Andrew.

1

That was precisely why she couldn't make up her mind. Forgetting Andrew himself was not the goal, only leaving behind the pain of his loss. At a mere twenty-five years of age, and still in possession of her youthful beauty, Rosemary was unlikely to remain a widow for long. However, the idea of moving on with her life made the hole in her heart throb miserably. No other man could ever live up to the standard Andrew had set.

Stalwart and true, Rosemary's late husband had been a rose among the thorns. He'd supported the suffragette movement, encouraged Rosemary in any endeavor to which she aspired, and had rarely spoken so much as a harsh word to her. In fact, he'd seen the potential in her artistic ability and bucked tradition by insisting she take part in his work as a private investigator.

Andrew had been a man who appreciated a woman's unique perspective.

The hours they'd spent discussing cases—Andrew sprawled on the chaise longue in one corner and Rosemary sketching away at her easel in the other—were some of the happiest memories she had. Those memories were part of why redecorating the office presented such a conundrum.

She circled the room now, seeing ghosts in every corner until her gaze alighted on a large clock placed above the door. The audible click it made with each ticking of the second hand had always irritated Rosemary, and it was the one item in the room she would not be sad to see removed.

She bit her lower lip and glanced at a ladder-backed chair positioned against the wall adjacent to the door. Making up her mind this was the place to begin the transformation, Rosemary pushed the chair against the door, kicked off her patent-leather T-strap heels, and gathered her skirt around her knees. With a jerk, she heaved herself onto the chair and reached up towards the casing.

The tips of her fingers reached only the lower rim of the clock, and it took considerable effort to wrench the piece free of the nail on which it hung. With impeccable timing, Wadsworth attempted to reenter from the other side, knocking the door into the chair and sending Rosemary to the ground with a grunt.

"Oh, my lady, are you hurt?" Wadsworth exclaimed, his normally pink, chubby cheeks blushing bright red as he reached down to help his mistress. Rosemary's shoulders shook as she laid the miraculously unbroken clock down upon the carpet.

"Do you need me to summon Dr. Barrow?" The butler's voice wavered with concern, but then his spine straightened and his eyes narrowed. "Are you laughing, madam?"

Rosemary nodded, and after another few moments of silent laughter, she reached out a hand and allowed Wadsworth to raise her from the floor. "I'm perfectly fine, though perhaps a tiny bit hysterical." Another giggle emerged from between her lips and had Wadsworth's settling into a thin, unamused line.

"You could have been injured, my lady. Should you have wanted me to remove that clock, you had only to ask."

Had even this mild admonishment come from Rosemary's mother's butler, she would not have wasted a moment before sending him packing, in search of another post. However, since Wadsworth had been more than just a servant in Andrew's eyes, Rosemary allowed him a certain amount of leniency.

To hell with what her mother thought, anyway. Rosemary had long since realized they would never see eye to eye. Though she would do nothing that would bring public shame to the Woolridge family, she certainly had no intention of betraying her beliefs in the privacy of her own home.

"Oh, Wadsworth, stop your grumbling. I'm none the worse for wear. But I would like a cup of tea now if you don't mind. You can thank me later for sparing you the chore of winding that monstrosity."

"Of course." He exited, taking a surreptitious look around before doing so as if searching for any other decorative pieces upon which his mistress might injure herself.

While she waited, Rosemary busied herself by drawing a sketch of the office as she envisioned it when completed. The room looked smaller than its actual dimensions due to a folding screen she and Andrew had picked out during a holiday to the Amalfi coast. Stowing it in a corner allowed for a proper assessment of the room's potential.

"Needs more light," she muttered. "Replace the heavy curtains with sheer fabrics." Yes, with the proper furnishings and decor, the walls would hold enough pieces to justify the room as a proper gallery.

Calculating the cost of such an endeavor, Rosemary jotted a list of the necessary changes. Her nose scrunched as she imagined writing out the number of cheques it would take to finance the endeavor. Since there was no one there, she needn't admit to feeling guilty about the idea of redecorating a room that had been furnished relatively recently and gently used.

If it means I don't have to avoid this space, it's worth it, she thought. The money was not a factor as Andrew had left her with enough to cover her living expenses for the foreseeable future. Even with paying the staff—Wadsworth, her lady's maid, Anna, housekeeper, and cook—Rosemary could live comfortably without using a penny of the stipend her parents had set aside for her. Should she decide to dip into those funds, however, redecorating the office wouldn't make a dent in the amount.

Rosemary deeply appreciated being solvent enough to do what she pleased, but would never be one to throw her money around like many of her generation. A penny saved is a penny earned, Andrew had always insisted.

To ensure she knew how to take care of herself, he'd included her when it came time to choose investments or pay bills. The value of money was something with which Rosemary was well acquainted, and she had no intention of wasting any of hers.

Where is that tea? Rosemary wondered when a sufficient amount of time had passed, and Wadsworth remained absent. She opened the office door and climbed the short set of stairs that led into a covered hallway housing both an exit to the street and an entrance into the house proper. The fervent sound of a woman's voice lilted towards her, along with the lower register of Wadsworth's replies.

"Miss, I do wish I could help you, but you see, Lillywhite Investigations is closed. Permanently." The word 'permanently' sent grief shuddering through Rosemary's chest, but what affected her more was the intensity of the woman's cries.

"Please, let me talk to Mr. Lillywhite. I'm certain we can work out some kind of arrangement," she begged.

"Unfortunately Mr. Lillywhite is …" Wadsworth grumbled, reluctant to say the words neither of them wanted to believe were true.

"What my butler is trying to say," Rosemary said, circling around Wadsworth's back and veritably shoving him aside, "is that my husband, Andrew Lillywhite, is no longer with us. So you see, there's no Lillywhite Investigations without him." She kept her tone matter-of-fact while she surveyed the woman standing on the doorstep.

Beneath a fresh application of powder, her nose was red and blotchy, and her eyes were ringed with a touch of kohl that failed to hide that she'd been crying. Aside from that, the woman looked about Rosemary's age and wore a drop waist dress that did nothing to detract from an enviably slim waistline.

"My apologies, Mrs. Lillywhite, I had no idea. I'm so sorry to have bothered you." The woman turned and bustled down the steps, and Rosemary nearly raced to follow before she realized she still wasn't wearing her shoes.

"Wait, Miss—" she called. The woman turned and returned to the doorstep with an uncertain look upon her face.

"It's Barton. Grace Barton." The name Barton struck Rosemary as vaguely familiar, but she couldn't place it from memory.

"Hello, Miss Barton. Would you please come in and join me for a cup of tea?" Rosemary gave Wadsworth a pointed glance, indicating that not only ought he to retrieve the tray but also provide them with some privacy.

Grace hesitated and then nodded and followed Rosemary into the office. Since his death, Andrew Lillywhite's widow had refrained from sitting in the chair behind his desk, but with a would-be client in the office, she considered for a moment then chose to simply sit next to Grace on the other side of the desk.

"Would you like to tell me what has you so upset?" Rosemary asked conversationally.

For a moment, she wondered if Grace would refuse to confide in her, but eventually, the words tumbled from her lips. "It's my father. I think his life is in danger. I didn't know where else to turn, so I came here. You see, I met your husband on a train back from Lyon. He gave me his card, which I never imagined I'd have reason to use. He seemed like a good man. I'm so sorry for your loss."

"He was, and thank you." Rosemary was grateful she hadn't had to ask Grace how the two had met, and vaguely remembered him telling her about a woman on the train a few weeks before his untimely death. Not that she'd suspected anything untoward; Andrew had been a proper gentleman in every way.

5

It was more that meeting someone who had known her husband made her feel closer to him, and yet somehow even further away. The notion that people were walking around with stories about Andrew that she would never hear made her sad—and, at the same time happy, for that meant he lived on in memory.

Choking back her emotion because this certainly wasn't the time for it, Rosemary gently prodded Grace until she had the details she needed. Mr. Barton had received a letter—the worst kind of letter—from an unknown source threatening his life. Rosemary was intrigued but unsure how to respond considering the investigative business was closed for good.

Still, she found herself asking all the important questions just as Andrew would have done.

"Was there a request for money in the letter?" Blackmail would be a simple solution; it usually was, because the blackmailer often succumbed to greed and gave himself away.

Grace sighed. "No, that's the odd part. It was just a threat, which is even worse. If they wanted something, Father could just give it to them, and this whole thing would be over. What kind of person does something like this?" she wailed.

Rosemary pulled a handkerchief from her pocket and passed it to the sobbing woman. "This type of thing happens all too often. Sadly, it's quite likely someone close to him. A business associate, possibly."

Or a family member, Rosemary thought to herself but didn't say out loud. "Did you happen to bring the letter with you?"

"No," Grace said. "I wouldn't dare remove anything from Father's desk drawer."

"That was probably for the best," Rosemary agreed, though she wished she had been given a chance to examine the letter. One could tell a lot from analyzing handwriting and, as an artist, the study of loops and whorls was something of a specialty of hers.

"Whatever shall I do?" Grace asked, the panic fading from her voice. All Rosemary heard now was resignation. "I felt as though coming here was my only hope. Father would either skin me alive or cut me off if he were to find out I'd gone behind his back like this."

That was a sentiment Rosemary could wholeheartedly understand. Some men felt that women were meant to look attractive and keep their mouths shut. Both were feats Rosemary frequently found herself

6

unable to manage. It seemed deferring to a man wasn't one of Grace's strengths, either.

"I shall simply return to Pardington and pray that nothing terrible happens before I gather the nerve to talk with Father," Grace stated miserably.

"Pardington? Are you one of the Bartons who lives at Barton Manor?" Rosemary asked, suddenly realizing why she had recognized the name.

Grace nodded. "Yes, I am."

"Well, then the saying about this being a small world has once again proved to be true. My maiden name is Woolridge," Rosemary explained.

The other woman appeared somewhat flummoxed and cast an odd look at Rosemary. "Your family is on the guest list for my parents' wedding anniversary celebration this weekend. I do not, however, know the status of their RSVP."

Several thoughts raced through Rosemary's mind. The first being she wanted to help Grace, but the second left her with a sense of uncertainty. Her parents had respected Andrew's line of work grudgingly, the large inheritance he had received from an elderly uncle having softened the blow.

They could not understand why a man of means would continue working at all, much less in a job that did not come with a high-level salary. Furthermore, they worried about Andrew's safety, as investigative work entailed a certain amount of risk.

Weighing the pros and cons of getting involved even marginally, particularly with a case adjacent to her parents' home, Rosemary made a quick decision. She had to admit she was intrigued, and it couldn't hurt to take a quick trip to Pardington and poke around a bit.

Should she feel there was a legitimate threat to Mr. Barton's life, she would advise Grace to alert the police and wash her hands of the whole affair.

"I'll help however I can. But remember, I'm not licensed and I can't get involved in any official capacity." She found herself making a promise she'd never intended to make, but since she'd given it, she'd uphold it if for nothing more than to honor Andrew's memory.

"Thank you, thank you so much."

7

CHAPTER TWO

Nervous, Rosemary paced back and forth across her bedroom while Anna bustled about, packing a case for the weekend in Pardington. Despite enjoying the soft feel of thick carpet beneath still-bare toes, Rosemary took a seat at the dressing table that matched a set of art deco drawers on the opposite wall.

She slid on a pair of thick stockings even though spring had turned the weather from rain and dreariness to a comfortable warmth that was a promise of the summer heat to come.

"Which dress are you wanting to wear to the party, my lady?" Anna asked, gesturing to a wardrobe filled to bursting with sensible black frocks. Her guarded expression held a smidgen of doubt that annoyed Rosemary no end, if for no other reason than it was justified. Her wardrobe was in serious need of a change, as she'd continued to don her mourning garb for months longer than the current custom.

"Pack a selection, and I'll choose one when I arrive," Rosemary replied. Anna still appeared at a loss, and her mouth opened and shut while a slight blush crept into her cheeks.

"Out with it, Anna," Rosemary gently prodded.

The girl raised an eyebrow but responded nonetheless. "Perhaps you ought to call on Miss Vera. She might have something more…appropriate for a party."

Rosemary grinned, "You know perfectly well giving Vera free rein over my wardrobe will result in my attending this party looking like I belong in a West-End brothel. However, I need a buffer, and Vera more than qualifies. Mother will have a fit, but that's half the fun."

"Shall I send word?" Anna asked with a small smile. The young woman had been in Rosemary's service since the beginning of her marriage to Andrew and had provided much comfort to her mistress in the months following his death. Rosemary didn't know what she'd do without Anna and treated the girl accordingly whether the gesture conformed to normal servant-mistress relationships or not.

"Yes, please do. Tell her to hurry, and to pack for all contingencies. She'll know exactly what to do," Rosemary instructed and sent Anna off to make arrangements.

While the maid was gone, Rosemary finished readying herself and slipped a framed photograph of Andrew into the inner pocket of her case along with a sketch pad and a few pencils. Trusting Anna to take care of the rest upon her return, Rosemary exited to the hall. She avoided the direction that led to her late husband's rooms and instead descended the stairs and settled herself in the dining room.

As soon as she'd taken a seat, a tray of toast and tea appeared at her side almost silently. She absently thanked the housemaid, who responded with a clipped "Madam," as was her custom. Of all the servants, Rosemary cared the least for Helen, whose veneer she had as yet been unable to crack.

She let a piece of buttered toast melt on her tongue and allowed a satisfied sigh to escape her lips. It had been difficult not to smother her sadness with biscuits and crisps, but she'd listened to her best friend Vera's advice for once and had managed to maintain her figure.

Yes, Vera had helped her in many ways, and not just over the last year. A force of nature, Vera took every opportunity to thumb her nose at convention. Even as children, when the pair had played endless games of make-believe, there couldn't have been a better example of two polar opposites.

Rosemary's dreams had included a husband, children, and a level of stability Vera described as 'boring in the extreme.' While her friend dreamt of excitement and stardom, always demanding to be the center of attention, Rosemary was happy to fade into the background.

She might not share Vera's enthusiasm for everything and anything that resembled fun, but she could understand the desire to break out of society's mold. The problem for Rosemary was that she cared about her family's approval far too much to be branded an embarrassment in any way. On the rare occasions that Vera talked her into defying custom, Rosemary had always been careful not to stray too far from convention.

The doorbell chimed as she swallowed the last dregs of her tea. Seconds later, Vera breezed into the dining room looking as though she'd been prepared for an impromptu weekend away long before Anna had summoned her.

A short crop of coal-black hair fit neatly beneath a stylish cloche hat, setting off a pair of emerald eyes surrounded by thick lashes. Her dress was cut to the most fashionable length, several inches shorter than anything Rosemary owned or dared to wear.

Rosemary looked enviously at Vera's lightly covered legs and fought the urge to remove her own itchy, uncomfortable stockings and rip them to shreds. Sometimes she wondered how such a creature had any use for her at all.

Surely, Vera could find more entertaining friends here in London, but for some unfathomable reason, she preferred Rosemary's company to that of anyone else.

"Rosie, you look absolutely invigorated. What's this about heading off to Pardington? If you wanted to get away, you could have chosen a nice sandy beach somewhere, my love. Going home to visit our parents isn't exactly top on my list of enjoyable activities."

Vera kissed Rosemary on the cheek, taking a break from her diatribe to do so. "You must have something up your sleeve if it means trudging out to the country with practically no forewarning."

Rosemary's eyes clouded over for a moment at the thought of what she was about to do. "I have an ulterior motive, yes," she hedged.

Vera let out the tinkling laugh that had beckoned many a man to her side, "I knew it. Spill," she demanded, collapsing into the chair across from Rosemary.

"I had a visitor yesterday. Grace Barton, from Pardington. She was looking for assistance from Andrew, and before she left, I somehow found myself saying I'd come out to the country and see if I could help her." Rosemary explained Grace's worry about her father, and the letter she'd found in his desk.

"I was just about to ask Wadsworth to move Andrew's desk, so I could begin converting the office, and it felt like serendipity when she said she was from Pardington. I know, it sounds like a terrible idea, but I couldn't seem to help myself."

Laughing again, Vera tossed her head and cast her friend an appraising look. "I do believe you have surprised me yet again, Rosie. Each time I start to believe you're a sad case and maybe there's no hope for you, you rise from the ashes like a phoenix and take me completely by surprise."

Rosemary highly doubted that was the case and chalked it up to Vera's theatrical nature. She was, after all, an aspiring actress. "I will simply carry out a consultation, and then I'll recommend the proper authorities."

"Whatever you say, darling," Vera replied, the corner of her lip still curled into a half grin. "We'll go to Pardington, we'll attend this party, and I have no doubt you'll have old Grace squared away before tea on Sunday."

"Old Grace?" Rosemary asked, her curiosity piqued. It wouldn't surprise her to learn that Vera knew the woman; after all, Vera knew practically everyone who was anyone, and a whole host of characters who would, in polite society, be considered nobodies.

"You must remember her; the Bartons are one of the most prominent families in Pardington."

Searching her memory, Rosemary came up empty. Perhaps the details would come back to her as she spent more time with the woman. "No, I don't, but it doesn't matter. Mother and Father will attend the party—presumably your mother as well—and that gives us an opportunity to poke around without seeming out of place. I'll need you to act as a distraction and also as an extra pair of eyes." Vera was nothing if not astute, and she possessed an uncanny ability to read any room she entered within seconds.

"Of course, of course. Whatever you need. If nothing else, the food ought to be delicious and the drinks bottomless. Besides, if I get bored, there's always your mother to torture with tales of my more deplorable acting jobs."

"Be careful," Rosemary laughed. "You know her patience only extends so far, and only so long as *your* mother is around. I swear, if Lorraine Blackburn told my mother that bald heads on women were coming into fashion, she'd turn up having been shorn like a sheep."

Vera's expression turned to one of evil satisfaction. "Wouldn't that be just the berries?"

Rosemary imagined her mother without hair, and the thought made her shiver with both amusement and discomfort. "No. In fact, it gives me the heebie-jeebies. Enough about that. Did you bring me something to wear? Something appropriate, I hope."

Eyes alighting with delight, Vera nodded emphatically. "I certainly did, and you will look absolutely ravishing. I also brought some jewelry. You must let me do something about that hair though, Rosie."

It would have been pointless to argue, and for the first time in a long time, Rosemary found she didn't really want to. It felt good to have a project, something to work towards. Of course, she'd much rather not be involved with a possible murder, but she would take what she could get.

"Maybe a nice bob. You could pull it off, with those cheekbones and your beautiful wide eyes..." While Rosemary mused, Vera had risen and crossed the room. With gentle hands, she scooped the honeyed length and scrunched it on top to measure different styles against Rosemary's face.

"Now wait just a second, I'm not bobbing my hair." That was where Rosemary had drawn the line. "Andrew always liked it long, and I agree."

Vera looked as though she wanted to say something about that, but resigned herself to bringing up the matter at a later date. "Then how about we put it up like we did the night you met? Those curls suited you nicely." She held her breath, hoping that had been the right thing to say.

She sighed when Rosemary responded with a smile. "That'll do just fine." Leave it to Vera to bring up a memory that normally would have Rosemary crying into her handkerchief, and yet somehow made everything a little brighter.

Fondly, Rosemary recalled the night in question, of the first time she'd locked eyes with Andrew after being dragged to a party nearly kicking and screaming. The whole world had become a little brighter that night, and it was nice to think of it without sadness for the first time in nearly a year.

Yes, Vera was a good egg—and a good friend—no matter what Rosemary's mother thought.

"Wadsworth," Rosemary called, certain the butler was hovering somewhere nearby, "please fetch Anna and load the luggage into the car. We're headed to Pardington."

Chapter Three

As the car pulled into the drive of Woolridge House, a mild sense of dread washed over Rosemary. Her childhood home carried many happy memories; her parents had taken pride in giving their children the finer things. Still, there was pain associated with the place that only partially had to do with the fact she and Andrew had been married there.

Vera, always intuitive to Rosemary's needs, gave her hand a sympathetic squeeze. She had her own demons to deal with, and Rosemary returned the gesture in acknowledgment of them.

"I'll see you later on tonight," Vera promised. She would stay just up the road at her mother's estate house, and Rosemary doubted she'd get any closer to Woolridge House than the front garden.

While Anna and Wadsworth, who had insisted upon accompanying his mistress as her driver, took care of the luggage, Rosemary made her way into the entrance hall. The pitter-patter of little feet met her ears, and a moment later she was nearly knocked over by a towheaded child who launched himself into her arms. "Auntie Rose, where'd you come from?"

"I came from my home in London, little darling. How's my favorite nephew?" she asked, kissing the chubby pink cheeks of her sister's son. "Where is your mother?" she asked, not having expected to encounter Stella, who spent most of her time at her husband's home in Oxford.

"In the dining room with Gran, I think. What did you bring me?" he asked, his blue eyes sparkling.

Rosemary sighed internally. "Well, Nelly, I didn't know you would be here," she began, hesitating when his adorable face fell. Thank goodness she'd packed a box of chocolates in her case. "However, Auntie always comes prepared. You'll get your present after tea."

The little boy, who was quickly approaching his fourth birthday, narrowed his eyes in consideration. "All right. Now, let's go." He took Rosemary's hand in his tiny one and led her towards the dining room.

"That is absurd!" She heard her mother, Evelyn's, voice before they'd rounded the corner. "You don't go to Paris in August, dear. It's far too humid. You go to Spain. Really, I don't know what you could possibly be thinking."

Rosemary thought Paris sounded like a marvelous place to visit but was certain if Stella had said she was taking a Spanish holiday, their mother would tell her she ought to go to France. That was the way things had always been between her mother and sister.

Stella followed every bit of advice Evelyn had given. She'd married young to an up-and-coming architecture professor, no less, and began having babies right away. She dressed the way Evelyn thought she ought to dress, and she decorated her home the way Evelyn instructed her to.

Yet, their mother still found fault with everything from Stella's shoes to her wallpaper, including Leonard, who, as far as Rosemary could tell, had done nothing except treat her sister with respect.

Still, for some reason, Stella continued to seek Evelyn's approval at all costs. It baffled Rosemary no end. Her own relationship with their mother might be strained at times, but she'd charted her path and taken little criticism for her deviation from the family's expectations.

Announcing her intention of going for an art degree had felt like a rebellion to Rosemary, and yet the news had been received with far less rebuke than Stella would have encountered had it been she who had presented the idea.

"Stella!" Rosemary rushed to embrace her sister, who appeared grateful for the reprieve. Petite in the extreme, Stella bore little resemblance to Rosemary, save the shape of her pointed nose, a feature handed down from their mother's side of the family.

Her tiny face was like a doll's, and she possessed a type of beauty that seemed more fitting for an Arthurian heroine or a fairy-tale princess. Although one would be hard-pressed to find another soul who agreed with her, Rosemary had always felt plain by comparison.

"Rose, I had no idea you were coming!" Stella's relieved expression confirmed for Rosemary that she was a welcome interruption.

"Did you call ahead, dear? Or send a telegram? If I've missed another message, I'll need to find a new maid. Or perhaps give Bertram a good tongue-lashing," Evelyn said.

Wishing it had indeed been the butler, Bertram, who had answered the telephone because then she would have been assured her mother had received the message, Rosemary replied, "I spoke to Father, and he said he'd inform you of my arrival. Perhaps I ought to have called again. I'm sorry, Mother."

"That's not what I meant, dear. You're welcome anytime, you know that. Still, you ought to know better than to trust your father to relay any sort of information. Why, he likely forgot he'd spoken to you the moment he set down the receiver. How long will you be staying?" Evelyn Woolridge had a tendency to ramble.

"Just for the weekend," Rosemary said. "I'm to attend a party at the Barton residence tonight."

Her mother stared at Rosemary for a moment before she asked, "With whom, dear? I didn't realize you were still friendly with their daughter. Or is it that dashing son of theirs who has captured your attention?"

A flush crept up to Rosemary's cheeks, but her voice was steady when she replied.

"I recently became reacquainted with Grace Barton, and it was she who extended the invitation. I'll be attending with Vera." She refused to elaborate again on her lack of desire to search for a new husband, an explanation that always fell on deaf ears. Stella flashed her sister a mischievous grin from behind their mother's back, and it made Rosemary feel good to know at least one person was on her side.

"Vera is here as well? I spoke to her mother just yesterday, and she mentioned nothing about an impending visit." Evelyn looked worried about the idea that her heroine, Lorraine Blackburn, might have withheld information.

Not for the first time did Rosemary wonder whether her mother thought, as did everyone else, that the two were an odd pairing. Evelyn, while still a handsome woman, looked like a moth next to a butterfly when Vera's mother was around. Sort of the same way Rosemary felt around Vera if she were being honest.

"Relax, Mother. Coming home this weekend was a last-minute decision. Now, why does everyone keep telling me I ought to remember

Grace Barton?" The notion had been bothering Rosemary ever since Vera had brought it up. Actually, longer than that. From the moment Grace had revealed she was from Pardington, a memory too vague to pin down had niggled in Rosemary's brain.

Evelyn cast a long look at her daughter. "You were Girl Guides together the year you turned fifteen."

She needn't have said anything else and chose not to. Instead, her eyes clouded over and she turned on her heel, abruptly leaving Rosemary and Stella alone in the dining room.

"I really put my foot in my mouth this time, didn't I?" Rosemary asked, even though the question had been an innocent one.

Stella sighed. "Your transgressions are far less painful than mine. I thought naming the baby after Lionel would make her happy, but every time she says his full name, she gets that look in her eye."

"I've noticed," Rosemary agreed. "Lionel would have been properly chuffed to have young Nelly carry his name, and that's what you must remember. The boy's nature is a credit to his uncle, and to be fair, Mother dotes upon her grandson, so he's none the worse for her pain."

Lionel had been Rosemary's oldest brother, the firstborn son of Evelyn and their father, Cecil, and heir to the family fortune. Furthermore, he was the only man Vera had ever—and Rosemary feared would ever—love. His death in the war had devastated the family, and the subsequent loss of Andrew had left Rosemary feeling more than jaded.

"Let's not talk any more about it," Stella suggested. "Such is life and all that. Now, show me what you intend to wear to this party. Mother and Father and Frederick will also attend, but Leonard and I will stay behind with Nelly."

"I didn't realize our family fostered such close connections to the Bartons," Rosemary commented, ignoring the ever-present inquiry regarding her wardrobe choices. "Have you any idea what reason our brother would have for attending the party?" Frederick had taken the brunt of the repercussions of Lionel's death and had never lived up to the Woolridge expectations, which appeared to be a family theme.

Stella laughed. "Well, Father does business with Mr. Barton, and Mother is trying to marry Frederick off, once and for all. She thinks a good woman will mend his wanton ways, but I think she forgets what women are like these days. Not that I have anything negative to say about Grace. I hardly know the woman."

Rosemary merely raised an eyebrow. She was closer to Frederick than she was to Stella and knew far more about his life than their sister could ever suspect. He could handle his own love life; however, Rosemary was beginning to wish she had let Grace Barton continue down her front step and out of her life.

If she'd known how involved their families were, she might have kept her mouth firmly closed. Sleuthing around Barton Manor whilst accompanied by most of her family sounded like an exercise in frustration. Her mother would watch her like a hawk and offer an opinion regarding every move she made.

And yet, Rosemary couldn't walk away. She'd seen the concern in Grace's eyes and had firsthand experience of what losing a family member could do to a person. If there was any way to help Mr. Barton, to prevent anything from happening to him, she'd do it whether or not her family approved.

Besides, she had Vera on her side, and if there was one truth in the world, it was that Vera could distract a hungry lioness from a weak gazelle with barely a modicum of effort.

Stella's right, Rosemary thought, *such is life.*

Chapter Four

Cecil and Evelyn Woolridge were to take their own car to Barton Manor, with Rosemary sticking to her plan of dressing at Vera's and driving over from there. "We cannot arrive too early, dear," her mother had said as though it had been she who had coined the phrase 'fashionably late.' Rosemary assumed Frederick would also arrive separately, as she had yet to see neither hide nor hair of him.

As Rosemary headed towards the door, her father descended the stairs looking as though he'd fallen asleep at his office table. She was almost positive the white indentation on his rosy cheek was in the shape of a paper clip.

Evelyn rounded the corner and caught sight of him. "There you are. You simply must get dressed, darling," she said, as though she had forgotten her previous statement regarding their planned arrival time.

"Yes, yes, Evelyn." Cecil hushed his wife with a wave of his hand. "All in due time. First, I'd like to say hello to my daughter, if you don't mind."

"Of course, of course. I only meant that—" Evelyn began.

Her husband interrupted gently. "I know what you meant, dear."

The look he cast at his wife expressed the high regard in which he held her. Rosemary had always appreciated that, despite how anyone else viewed her mother, she continued to hold Cecil's affections even after decades of marriage.

Her father was a gentleman, a scholar at heart, and a businessman by necessity. Having inherited a depleted fortune, he had done quite well for himself, restoring the family name through good old hard work and determination.

Rosemary gave her father a kiss on each cheek, accepted the adoring look in his eyes when he gazed at her, and quickly exited once he had tottered off to ready himself for the party.

Upon arriving at Vera's, a butler she didn't recognize greeted Rosemary—Lorraine Blackburn went through staff at an alarming rate—and directed her up the lavish marble staircase that was as familiar to her as her own entrance hall. Rosemary and Vera had met at school, fallen in love with one another, and inspired a friendship between their mothers that was almost as strong as their own.

At the time, Mrs. Blackburn had been a shell of her fabulous self. Now, having lost a husband, Rosemary understood far more about the woman's state of mind than she had as a child.

They had all lost, but both Blackburn women had taken the pain and turned it into an otherworldly strength of character that most people didn't recognize as a coat of armor. Often accused of callousness, Vera followed her mother's example and let the opinions of most roll off her back like inconsequential raindrops.

Now, Vera stood before a large gilt-framed mirror and twirled around as she saw Rosemary approaching. Her expression changed from a welcoming smile to a look of absolute horror when she took in Rosemary's outfit.

"Undress immediately. You are not wearing funeral garb to an anniversary party. In fact, when we get back to London, I'm coming over to clean out your wardrobe. Now, you go into my dressing room and put this on." She handed Rosemary a hanger with far too little material clinging to it, and pointed toward the door, "No arguments."

"As if arguing would make any difference, except to our arrival time," Rosemary joked with a laugh as she took the proffered garment. "Fine, fine, I'll be out in a minute," she promised after noting the raised eyebrow Vera shot her way.

Once she was alone, she took a minute to look at the fringed frock her friend had chosen. Still black, but with a far more daring neckline than the one she'd brought with her, it hugged her slim hips in all the right places while showing a moderate amount of sheer black-stockinged leg.

A triple strand of pearls and rhinestones covered enough of her décolletage for her to remain appropriate, and a pair of black, diamante-accented pumps with a Cuban heel completed the ensemble.

Vera pushed into the dressing room and surveyed her friend. "Here, I have earrings and a bracelet to match." She sat Rosemary down at a cluttered dressing table, rolled her hair into perfect finger waves, and added more kohl to her eyes to create a smoky effect. "Now, you look absolutely perfect!"

"Next to you, I will always look like a canceled stamp. Though tonight, perhaps, I won't be pegged for a spinster." Andrew would want Rosemary to be happy, and feeling attractive—in her own way, at least—let her shrug off some of the mantle of sadness constantly draped over her shoulders.

Smoothing her hands down the front of her dress, Rosemary cautioned her friend. "Remember, Vera, this isn't just a social call. We're trying to find out whatever we can about Mr. Barton's death threat. This is serious business."

"Yes, I know, my love. I am at your service." Vera dipped into a dainty curtsy, and Rosemary couldn't help but let loose another smile.

\#

\#

Barton Manor sat atop an expanse of rolling hills, and the driveway snaked through an elaborate garden that had just burst into bloom. Daffodils, peonies, and tulips lined the path and grew here and there in strategically placed clumps. The steeple of a small chapel visible in the distance contributed to the charming atmosphere.

Giving the impression they were guarding the manor, a pair of sculptured topiaries in the shape of lions flanked the gate. Rosemary suddenly remembered having seen those lions before and decided she would have a personal conversation with Grace at the first opportunity.

Had Grace recognized her as an old acquaintance when she'd arrived at Lillywhite Investigations, and if so, why hadn't she said something at the time?

Moreover, why couldn't Rosemary remember Grace? The hole in her memory was becoming worrisome.

"A bit pretentious, don't you agree?" Vera said under her breath as if her home wasn't just as elegant. Yet, there was something about Barton Manor that *did* appear pretentious, just as Vera had pointed out.

Pursing her lips, Rosemary attempted to quantify the difference. Both properties boasted meticulously groomed lawns fading back to several copses of trees, sharply edged gardens in spring bloom, with many-roomed mansions as the centerpiece. The difference might lie, she mused, in the pink-shading-to-red blooms in the gardens. Lorraine preferred a riot of cheerful color to a rigid palette.

20

Then again, it might have been the presence of a small grouping of headstones surrounded by an iron fence that ruined the symmetry of the view and lent a slightly sinister air. Rosemary couldn't imagine why anyone would want to situate a house adjacent to a graveyard, no matter how quaint the chapel grounds might appear from a distance.

"It lacks a welcoming feel; that much is certain. Though the view of the hillside is enviable," Rosemary murmured.

Vera's driver maneuvered the car to a stop and held the rear door open for his mistress and her friend. A stoic butler clad in a crisp black tailcoat with a starched white shirt opened the door before anyone could knock, and took their names.

"Please follow me to the ballroom, ladies." He walked briskly through an elegant entrance hall and towards the sounds of music emanating from a room at the end of a long hallway.

Rosemary glanced at the family portraits that lined the wall along the entrance hall, recognizing a younger Grace surrounded by two people who Rosemary guessed to be Mr. and Mrs. Barton, and an attractive boy on the cusp of manhood.

On the other side of the entrance, a door opened, and a man ducked out of it. Everything about him could be described as medium, from his stature and build to the color of his brown hair and matching suit. His eyes darted around the room before landing on Rosemary and Vera. He pasted a smile on his face and made his way toward them.

"Mr. Cuthburt, you are aware that the rest of the manor is closed off for the party, are you not?" The butler said, his tone icy.

Mr. Cuthburt let out a husky laugh and nearly managed to suppress an eye roll. "Yes, Geoffrey, my good man. I think the fact that I am a regular visitor to Barton Manor ought to grant me some leniency, don't you agree?"

It was a challenge, and one to which Geoffrey had no intention of rising. "Of course, Mr. Cuthburt. Ladies, the ballroom is through there," he said in a clipped tone before taking his leave.

Rosemary and Vera ignored the awkward situation and followed Mr. Cuthburt's unimpressive figure through the entrance.

CHAPTER FIVE

Twinkling chandeliers lit the ballroom with a golden glow, and as Rosemary and Vera entered, a waiter dressed just as formally as the butler offered flutes of champagne. In one corner, a live band played a jaunty tune that invited one to tap a foot to the beat.

Rosemary felt a hand on her shoulder and turned to see Grace Barton looking significantly more composed than she had two days before, though there was a tightness around her eyes to attest she still had a lot on her mind

"Hello, Grace, what a lovely party. I hope you don't mind that I brought Vera Blackburn along."

"Of course I don't, Mrs. Lillywhite," she said. "The more, the merrier."

"Grace, please, I think we're past the point of formality considering we have a history," Rosemary said and left it at that. Andrew's words echoed in her head, *Never offer up more information than you must. Insinuate and then wait. Let them come to you.* He'd been speaking of a suspect, and Grace was hardly that. Still, the same rules applied.

The woman blushed and looked between Vera and Rosemary as though embarrassed. "I didn't mean to mislead you. In fact, I didn't realize who you were until after I'd left your flat. I hope you understand." Grace looked shyly in Vera's direction, and Rosemary recognized her expression.

She'd seen it on the children with whom she'd attended school, on the men who watched Vera's performances with bated breath, and on the few women who had enough self-confidence not to be intimidated by her brilliance.

The rest, convinced she was a snake in the grass just waiting to pick off their beaus, tended to regard Vera with jealousy-laced malice.

22

If Rosemary wasn't mistaken, Grace idolized Vera and would have liked to be her friend.

"It's perfectly okay. I didn't recognize you, either. I hope you didn't take offense," Rosemary replied.

Grace shook her head. "No, none at all. I know how difficult our school years were for you, and it's not as though we were terribly close."

Bits and pieces of memory swam up from the depths of Rosemary's subconscious, and with the puzzle falling into place, she finally pulled the image of a younger Grace to the surface.

Quiet and shy, Grace had been a girl who had always followed the rules and therefore had few friends. Of course, that was years ago. In all likelihood, she had changed since then. Most people did.

Once the appropriate pleasantries had been exchanged, Grace, taking a surreptitious look around as she did, led Rosemary and Vera out of the ballroom and into the hallway where they could talk privately.

"The way I see it, whoever wrote that note is probably here tonight. Father has invited a whole host of his business associates and several close friends. It's a place to start, anyway. Later, we'll sneak away and look at the letter."

"Perfect," Rosemary replied. "For now, I'd like to observe everyone present as well as your father, so I think it would be best if we mingled. Keep your eyes open for anything out of the ordinary, or anyone—besides us—who wasn't on the guest list."

Over Grace's shoulder, Rosemary spotted her mother and father engaged in a lively conversation with the guests of honor. "Introduce us around a little, and then we can split up."

"All right, but let's meet back here once Father has given his toast. They'll dance, and then we can slip out," Grace suggested as she parted the crowd and approached the group.

"Cecil, you old dog," Mr. Barton boomed. "You know how much business gets done on the golf course. Why can't I convince you to join the club? I play with Arthur and Ernest every Wednesday, and it's been well worth the monthly fee."

Mrs. Barton placed a hand on Evelyn's arm. "By all means, send Cecil off to chase the little white ball. Take the free time to go to the spa. I recommend the muscle-lifting treatment. As you can see, it took five years off my face. You *must* try one, I insist."

The words alone could have been taken as a friendly suggestion, but something in the tone of Mrs. Barton's voice turned them into an underhanded insult. Come to think of it, the way Mr. Barton had spoken to her father was enough to make Rosemary take an immediate dislike to the man.

It wasn't the first time she'd been put in a position where a client's personality rubbed her up the wrong way, and so she shoved her opinions away and vowed to approach this case with an open mind. Just because the Bartons were utter snobs didn't mean Mr. Barton deserved to be murdered.

"Grace, please fetch me another glass of champagne," Mrs. Barton ordered her daughter, the words dripping like honey but with a sharp edge that caused Rosemary's eyes to narrow. Grace's face turned a discomfited shade of red, but she said nothing and scurried off to do her mother's bidding.

"I'll have my girl pencil you in for this week, Cecil. I insist." Mr. Barton was still carrying on about golf, much to the displeasure of her father.

Mr. Woolridge merely smiled, and Rosemary guessed it wasn't the first time he had been forced to deal with the likes of men such as Mr. Barton. "Not my cup of tea, Edgar. Not my cup of tea at all. Oh, hello, Rosemary. You look..." He faltered.

"You look lovely, dear." Evelyn cut in. The twinkle in her eye let Rosemary know she'd made a misstep. Wearing Vera's fashionable dress had only served as ammunition for her mother's theory she'd come here to nab herself a man. "Eva, Edgar, this is our daughter, Rosemary. I believe she's friends with Grace."

"Hello, hello." Edgar Barton nodded, his eyes sliding just south of Rosemary's neckline. She fought back the urge to say something saucy and instead allowed him to kiss her hand even though the feel of his lips on her skin made her stomach churn.

"And this is Rosemary's friend, Vera Blackburn," Evelyn continued as if she hadn't noticed Rosemary's discomfort. Whether or not her mother intended it, introducing Vera took the attention off Rosemary completely, which was just fine with her. Vera was used to older men fawning over her and took Mr. Barton's admiration in her stride.

The same couldn't be said for his wife, who eyed Vera with venom in her eyes. It looked as though her husband was about to make another unwelcome comment when a handsome man approached the group, his eyes fastened on Rosemary in a far less obnoxious manner than Mr. Barton's had done.

"Theodore, where have you been all evening?" Mrs. Barton asked while Rosemary tried to dislodge Vera's elbow from her ribs. Never one to employ subtlety, Vera's gaze flicked from Rosemary to the man named Theodore with a suggestive eyebrow wiggle. "You know Mr. and Mrs. Woolridge, and this is their daughter Rosemary and her friend, Vera Blackburn," Mrs. Barton continued.

Theodore smiled an enigmatic smile and took Rosemary's hand while nodding to Vera, "It's a pleasure, Miss Woolridge."

"Actually, it's Mrs. Lillywhite," Rosemary said automatically, and then blushed.

Her mother, unable to allow such a specimen of a man to believe Rosemary unavailable, quickly jumped in to explain, "Our poor Rosemary is a widow."

"I'm very sorry to hear that," Theodore said, his eyes filled with sincerity, "and please, call me Teddy. Can I interest the two of you in accompanying me to the bar?"

Vera practically pushed Rosemary toward him, and they bade goodbye to the group as Theodore led them away with Rosemary's hand in his. He let go before the moment turned awkward, but that didn't help Rosemary's color return to normal.

"What's your poison? Actually, let me guess. It's a special talent of mine." Theodore gazed between Rosemary and Vera, rubbed his chin for a moment and then pointed towards Rosemary, "A classic G&T for you, possibly with a twist, and for your friend, I'm going with a Negroni. Was I close?"

Rosemary battled the urge to lie and say he was wrong, but a giggle she hadn't been expecting escaped her lips. "Yes, you're spot on. I will take that twist."

"Make mine a Boulevardier please," said Vera, "but I'll give you credit, that's a handy talent, especially at parties."

25

Teddy grinned, and Rosemary believed she could imagine exactly what he must have looked like as a child. "Here you go," he said, handing over the drinks. Rosemary took a sip and then held on to her glass. The last thing she needed was to get sloshed and miss out on a vital clue. Teddy Barton was distraction enough.

It looked as though he might have been preparing to ask her to dance when a velvety voice cut through the band's music. "Well, hello, Theodore," the voice purred. Rosemary whipped her head around to see who was speaking and her gaze landed on a spectacularly attractive woman wearing a dress that barely skimmed her thighs. Never one to enjoy being upstaged, Vera let out a huffing sound.

"Marjorie," Theodore answered in a dry tone that nearly elicited another giggle from Rosemary. If she wasn't mistaken, he didn't find the woman nearly as enchanting as Marjorie wished he did. "Meet Rosemary Lillywhite and Vera Blackburn. Ladies, Marjorie Ainsworth."

"Charmed, I'm sure." Marjorie flashed a faux smile toward Rosemary and Vera, turned her back to them, and spoke directly to Theodore as if they'd ceased to exist. "Come and dance with me, Teddy. Please?" Her long black lashes fluttered seductively, and her deep-blue eyes sparkled from beneath a blond fringe of finger curls that shone in the twinkling lights of the chandelier above.

She ran one manicured hand up Theodore's arm, pressing herself against him as much as she could and leaning in to give him an unobstructed view of her considerable assets. His chiseled jaw clenched with irritation, and his dark eyes turned stormy beneath a prominent brow. The expression ought to have made him appear formidable, but it only accentuated his good looks.

"I'm sorry, Marjorie, but I've just been told I'm needed elsewhere. I'll see you later. You too, ladies," Teddy said, shooting Rosemary an apologetic look and then nearly running off in the opposite direction. Vera was shaking with barely concealed laughter, and once again Rosemary resisted the urge to say something her mother would consider unladylike.

Marjorie stared after Teddy as though thoroughly baffled by his sudden departure, which only made the situation all the funnier.

As soon as Theodore had disappeared, a gainly, dark-haired gentleman approached Marjorie. He was attractive, or at least he believed he was. Yet there was something about his appearance that just seemed smarmy. Rosemary was sure he had been watching for Teddy's departure and had waited to approach the woman once she was alone.

"Hello there, Marjie. I saved you a dance. What do you say?" He held out a hand as if expecting her to fall into his arms.

Rosemary and Vera watched incredulously, thoroughly enjoying the show, as Marjorie snapped, "Go chase yourself, Herbie. You're such a sinker. Besides, shouldn't you be dancing with Grace? Remember Grace?" She stalked away, her nose in the air, and Herbie's face turned the color of roasted beetroot before he moved off in the other direction.

"I think I'll finish this now," Rosemary said, slugging back the rest of her G&T once they'd finished convulsing over Marjorie Ainsworth's bad fortune.

CHAPTER SIX

"I think I'm about to get my chance to slip out and meet Grace." Rosemary pointed toward where the band had stopped playing, and Ernest Cuthburt, the man from the entrance hall, took center stage. "Can you keep watch in case someone notices our absence?"

"Of course, but be careful poking around," Vera warned, turning her attention back to the stage.

The man cleared his throat before speaking. "Please forgive my interruption, but I'd like to say a few words about the couple we're here to celebrate tonight. For those of you who don't know me, I'm Ernest Cuthburt, and I have known the Bartons since their children were babies. I'm proud to say my godchildren, Theodore and Grace, are more family to me than my own."

That explained why he had felt comfortable enough to enter rooms the Bartons had wanted to remain free of guests, and also why he had so blatantly challenged the butler. Mr. Cuthburt clapped a hand to his friend's back, and Rosemary noted how very similar the two men were in appearance. Both wore suits of nearly identical color and style even if there was a noticeable difference in the quality.

Though Mr. Cuthburt had displayed behavior of a somewhat questionable nature, he appeared far more genial than Mr. Barton, and Rosemary decided that of the two she liked him far better than her host.

As Mr. Cuthburt continued extolling the virtues of the Bartons' marriage, Rosemary had to raise an eyebrow considering the way Mr. Barton had behaved right in front of Mrs. Barton. She seized the opportunity to look around and take stock of the crowd.

A few of the village ladies Rosemary recognized, and she could tell by the expressions on their faces and the way they kept glancing between Mr. and Mrs. Barton, that tomorrow, the gossip mill would churn at full speed. She highly doubted anything they had to say would be considered complimentary and felt sorry for Grace and Teddy. Both seemed like good people despite having been brought up by a couple who didn't appear to have endeared themselves to their neighbors.

Looking around, she noticed someone else who had her eyes trained on the stage. Marjorie Ainsworth's face was blank, though a muscle near her upper lip twitched slightly. When Mrs. Barton regarded her with a sneering glare, Marjorie dropped her hands to her sides, turned on her heel, and retreated towards the bar.

Observation is a sleuth's most useful tool, Andrew had always said, and he was correct. Rosemary was learning a lot about the situation at Barton Manor just by watching the way the guests interacted with their hosts. Nothing she'd seen painted the Bartons in the best light, but she wondered if jealousy over their wealth might have something to do with popular opinion. Deciding to hold out judgment, for the time being, she began planning her exit.

Rosemary waited until the guests applauded Mr. Cuthburt's speech before she seized the opportunity to slip out of the side door of the ballroom. Instead of finding Grace waiting for her, Rosemary was pleasantly surprised to encounter her brother, Frederick, who had been standing in the doorway watching Mr. Cuthburt give his toast with a cynical expression on his face.

"Rosie," he exclaimed, slinging an arm around his sister's shoulders.

"Hello, Freddie, I was wondering when you'd show up. Why did you want to come to this thing, anyway? It's not exactly your usual scene."

Blue eyes that perfectly matched hers crinkled as full lips turned up into a mischievous grin. "Now and then, I like a change of scenery."

"You mean Mother dragged you here hoping to pair you off with the most eligible woman she could find. I'm in the same boat," Rosemary lamented. "Shall I pass you an oar?"

Frederick elbowed her in the ribs. "In your case, it might be working. Don't think I didn't notice the look on your face when Theodore Barton passed you that drink. He's the most eligible bachelor in the room. Though I think I'm more handsome, in a rugged sort of way. Don't you agree?"

Rosemary rolled her eyes at her brother. "You are the most handsome, of course, Freddie." Indeed, her brother was handsome,

29

with his unruly curls and the aforementioned eyes, plus an air of unattainability that many women seemed to want to challenge.

Occasionally self-absorbed to the point of narcissism, Frederick was under the impression he would always come up short when compared with his older brother. Overcompensation, that was what drove Frederick, though his attitude grated on their father's nerves.

"And I'm not here to meet anyone," Rosemary continued. "I'm here to help Grace with a little investigating." Frederick would worm the truth out of her eventually anyway, and since she held more of his secrets than he'd like for her to have, he wouldn't dare bare any of hers to the world.

That did not also mean he wouldn't give her an earful of his opinion on the subject, however, and Rosemary prepared for an onslaught while she filled her brother in on the details. To her surprise, he said nothing, only pierced her with those blue eyes and nodded once.

"Say whatever it is you have to say, brother dear. I can take it."

"I'm not saying a word, Rose. In fact, I think a project might be exactly what you need. You're going to have to do this with my help, though, because there's no way I'm letting you put yourself in harm's way."

Since it was easier to let Frederick think he was indulging her whim, or worse, that he was supporting her in an endeavor meant to help her get over Andrew, she merely nodded and left him to his illusions.

"Have you seen Grace around?" Rosemary asked. "We agreed to meet once the toasts had begun, but she's not here."

Frederick shook his head, "No, but I'm not entirely certain which one she is. I've never met her before."

"I thought you knew these people, Freddie," Rosemary chided.

"Only Mr. Barton, and only in a business capacity. Limited business capacity, because Father still insists upon chaperoning me as though I were a two-year-old." Their father kept a tight hand on his business affairs, so much so that Rosemary had only a vague idea of what the family business entailed.

To finance the productions of the textiles sold by Woolridge & Sons, Cecil Woolridge had invested money in a variety of other companies, but the details were so seldom discussed that she had never given it much thought.

30

"She's wearing a sapphire cocktail dress with a fringe along the hem," Rosemary explained to her brother, "and this lovely little pair of—oh, never mind, just follow me." She led him into the ballroom and looked around for Grace.

Instead, her attention was captured when the main doors, the ones leading into the ballroom from the entrance hall, opened to frame Vera's mother in the doorway.

Lorraine Blackburn posed without seeming to pose in a sequined gown that was more than a touch too fancy for this occasion but sparkled in the light. She was even more lovely than Vera, and that was saying something.

Rosemary watched as her mother parted from the crowd and attached herself to the newcomer, following slightly behind like a puppy as Lorraine made her way towards the bar.

"Now the party officially begins," Frederick whispered conspiratorially to Rosemary. Every eye in the room seemed trained on Mrs. Blackburn; most of the men's wide with appreciation, while many of the women's narrowed to slits of envy.

Lorraine pretended not to notice even though it was clear she was used to—and enjoyed—the attention. Rosemary glanced around and fastened her gaze on Mrs. Barton, who glared at Mrs. Blackburn with barely concealed hatred.

"It seems there isn't a woman here who Mrs. Barton gets along with, including her daughter," Rosemary whispered back. "She looks like a snake, and Vera's mother is the poor mouse who doesn't understand she's about to be swallowed whole."

Frederick's cheeks pulled up into a grin. "I believe the viper will suffer quite a shock when she realizes Lorraine Blackburn has fangs of her own. Lorraine is the type of woman who is either loved or hated. There can be nothing in between. Come on, I need a drink." He led Rosemary towards the bar while she continued scanning the room for signs of Grace.

Herbert Lock, still attempting to get his hooks into Marjorie, was explaining a complicated drink recipe to the barman, and the look on his face when he turned around to find Frederick and Rosemary standing there was one of immense irritation.

31

"Hello there, Herbie," Frederick said as though he were speaking to a child in the playground. "Taking advantage of the stocked bar, I see." It didn't sound as though the idea surprised him.

Herbert scowled at Frederick, ignored Rosemary completely, then glanced between Marjorie and the dance floor as if making a silent suggestion. Her eyes trained on Frederick, she didn't spare Herbert another glance.

"And who might you be?" Marjorie asked in the same tone she had used with Theodore Barton, strengthening Rosemary's opinion that the woman was an opportunist looking for rich, handsome prey.

"This is my brother, Frederick Woolridge," Rosemary answered, amused by the look of sheer annoyance that passed across Marjorie's face when Frederick failed to supply a name. "Freddie, this is Marjorie Ainsworth."

"The famous Marjorie Ainsworth," Frederick boomed, pleased at the prospect of both annoying Herbert and being flirted with by a woman of Marjorie's caliber. She was lovely, at least when she was quiet and had a target in her sights. "I've heard a lot about you, you know. We don't get many newcomers way out here in Pardington, and it seems you've been making quite a splash with the locals."

Of course, she believes that to be a good thing, Rosemary thought to herself while Marjorie preened and leaned a little closer to Frederick. *How can she not recognize the insult?*

"I'm sure not even the wildest stories could have truly done me justice," Marjorie flirted shamelessly, "though, you could find that out for yourself if you were so inclined."

Frederick grinned, but earned himself a few good brother points when he replied, "I've got to make the rounds with my lovely sister first, but I might take you up on that later if I may."

Marjorie bit back a scowl and pasted a smile on her face, "Yes, that would be lovely." Her voice was tight, and when she noticed Herbert's smirk, she looked as though she wanted to punch him right there in the Bartons' ballroom.

"Well done, brother mine," Rosemary muttered to Frederick as she linked arms with him and began walking in the opposite direction. "Watch out for her, she's a man-eater if I ever saw one."

"Just the way I like them, Rosie. Just the way I like them."

Across the room, Rosemary spotted Vera wearing an expression of extreme boredom as she nodded along to whatever her companion was saying. As Grace had failed to appear, Rosemary pushed through the crowd and approached her friend, who shot her a look of gratitude and Frederick a narrow-eyed glare.

The last time Frederick had been in London, Vera had lost a rather sizable bet to him, though neither would reveal the specific terms. Money changed hands between those two on the regular, and when they were together, both of them acted as though they were still children and not fully grown adults.

"This is Mr. Arthur Abbot, an associate of Mr. Barton's," Vera explained. Rosemary was beginning to wonder if this party had been an excuse for Edgar Barton to gather all of his business partners in one place.

He didn't appear particularly excited about celebrating the thirtieth anniversary of his marriage to Mrs. Barton, and in fact, Rosemary hadn't seen the feted couple together since the beginning of the evening.

Not even during Mr. Cuthburt's speech had Mrs. Barton stood with her husband. Perhaps she had also realized her anniversary party was a farce.

Come to think of it, Rosemary realized she had lost sight of Mr. Barton entirely. Another scan of the room revealed no brown-suited man. Dragging her attention back to the introduction at hand, she greeted the man who was now smiling at her as though she might be dim.

"Hello, Mr. Abbot," Rosemary replied politely. "Do you know my brother, Frederick Woolridge?"

"Not personally, no. I know your father, though. Good man, Cecil Woolridge," Mr. Abbot boomed. "I was just telling your friend here about my newest art acquisition," Abbot continued without waiting for anyone to reply. No wonder Vera had felt trapped—it didn't seem as though one could get a word in edgewise when Arthur Abbot had the floor.

While the man expounded upon the sublime beauty and resonant eloquence of a single brush stroke, all Rosemary could think about was the size and shape of the mole above his eyebrow. Two thick hairs sprouted from one end and made it look as though an overly large brown ladybird had landed upon the man's forehead and decided to take up residence there.

Fascinated, it wasn't until she heard Abbot mention the word "injection" that she was able to pull her attention back to the conversation.

It appeared he had moved on to another topic.

"Having to be under the care of a personal physician is an inconvenience, but I do believe the treatment will add years to my life. Worth it, eh?" An elbow shot towards Frederick's ribs, but he sidestepped handily, and, fixing his eyes upon a spot over Arthur Abbot's shoulder, feigned a look of resignation.

"Why, Rosemary, I believe we're being summoned. The mater and pater seem to need a word." To Arthur, he said, "Fascinating story, old chap. Must tell me how it all turns out." He gave the man a hearty thump on the back.

Before the daggers in Vera's eyes could turn lethal, Rosemary saved the day. "Vera, would you mind awfully if I tore you away for a moment?"

"Of course not, darling. Whatever you need." The three young people attempted to make their escape, while Abbot trailed behind, too thick to take the hint.

Rosemary finally spotted Grace who, in the midst of ducking out one of of the doors to the balcony spanning the exterior of the ballroom, turned sideways as she passed Mr. Cuthburt on his way back inside.

No, doing a double-take, Rosemary realized it was actually Mr. Barton, cheeks flushed from the cold and brow furrowed in what appeared to be irritation, who had just walked by his only daughter without sparing her a glance.

Rosemary poked Frederick in the side while Mr. Abbot, having returned to his former preoccupation, continued to wax on about how many paintings he had purchased from an up-and-coming artist in London. Normally, this was a conversation Rosemary could sink her teeth into, but for the moment she had more pressing concerns.

"Sorry, brother, I owe you one," she said low enough so only Frederick could hear, and with Vera in tow, mercilessly ditched him to Mr. Abbot's tender graces.

Chapter Seven

Once outside, Rosemary shivered in the chill that had crept into the fresh spring air now that the sun had set. She pulled her shawl around her shoulders and looked around for Grace.

Veering left, and following the curve of the balcony, she could see the outlines of party guests on the other side of the curtained windows. It reminded her of the theater, all the characters playing their respective roles, while she, as an observer, watched in silence. Except, it was as though she'd come in at the interval and missed the first act in its entirety.

This, to her, was a familiar sensation, one she'd experienced many times during an investigation, and it only piqued her curiosity. The desire to unravel the puzzle strengthened her resolve to learn who might be threatening the owner of Barton Manor.

Escalating voices pulled Rosemary out of her reverie, and she followed them until she could see Grace's shadow splayed across the stone floor just around the next bend.

"Come on, Grace. What I'm asking is easy dough to a man like your father. We know Teddy is in for the lion's share, so we need something to keep us rolling in the green for the rest of our lives. You and me, that's the plan, isn't it?" Rosemary recognized the whiny, grating tone of Herbert Lock's voice, and held her breath while she eavesdropped without remorse.

Grace recoiled slightly. "You know I haven't agreed to anything yet, and all this talk about money is making me uncomfortable. You obviously don't know my father as well as you think you do if you believe he would want you discussing such matters with his daughter. Furthermore, you aren't ingratiating yourself by pestering me about it. If you want an investor, ask Father yourself."

"Don't you think I already have?" Herbert snapped. "He claims his assets aren't liquid enough and I know it's a blatant lie."

"Whatever my father says, I believe to be true. Or, perhaps he has no desire to enter into an investment with you. Again, Herbert, if Father has already said no, then no is the answer. I wouldn't recommend interfering with him." It sounded like a threat to Rosemary and a well-deserved one.

Herbert bristled. "What exactly is that supposed to mean, Grace?" He sounded a little out of breath, as though the proverbial rug had been pulled out from beneath him.

"It means that I believe I have made my decision after all, and I've every intention of telling my father just what a cad you are. Do not expect him to continue to support you as a suitor, as I highly doubt he will appreciate your treatment of me. Nor your obvious attempts at digging for whatever gold you can siphon from him." She turned as if to go, and Herbert reached out and grabbed her by the elbow.

"Don't walk away from me." Suddenly, the whiny tone disappeared, and his voice sounded menacing. "You'll do what I ask, or *I* will talk to your father. I'll tell him what I saw in London, and then we'll see how he really feels about his precious little angel."

Rosemary's eyebrows lifted toward her forehead, and she stepped into the light to come to Grace's defense. Herbert appeared as though he'd swallowed a frog, and Grace's eyes looked dark in a face gone pale.

If Herbert was the violent type, Rosemary's presence would do little to dissuade him from action, but then again, he didn't know about the self-defense lessons she had had at her late husband's insistence.

"Grace, I need a word," Rosemary said, her voice clipped and her eyes bright enough to burn holes straight through Herbert Lock.

Grace extricated herself from Herbert's now-limp grasp and followed Rosemary inside. Neither woman said anything to the other until they had weaved their way through the crowd and into the back hallway where they had agreed to meet when the opportunity arose to slip away unnoticed.

"I'm so sorry you had to witness that," Grace said when they were alone.

Rosemary shook her head. "You have nothing to be sorry for. It's your business, and I shouldn't have slithered up on you like that."

"Thank goodness you did. Herbert isn't a bad man, but he has a temper," she explained. "He thinks he's entitled to my hand in marriage, but—" Grace continued until Rosemary cut her off.

"You don't love him." It was a statement, not a question, as Grace's tone had already conveyed the answer.

"No, I don't," Grace conceded. "But that doesn't always matter, does it?"

Shaking her head, Rosemary agreed. "It ought to, but I know it doesn't. Does your father know the extent of your dislike for the man? Has he seen this side of Herbert for himself?"

Grace sighed. "Father only ever sees what he wants to see. It is odd, though. Please don't think me conceited, but I'm not a frumpy woman, and my family is obviously wealthy. I'm not pining for marriage proposals, nor do I need to marry for money. Father has never thought any of my suitors were good enough. It seems ironic that he would finally decide upon someone I cannot tolerate."

"Yes, that is odd," Rosemary said, thinking some thoroughly deplorable thoughts about Mr. Barton. "But these things have a way of working themselves out. Ultimately, it's your decision." She could not yet tell if Grace was the type of woman who would rather be happy than rich, but she suspected as much.

"However, it will not matter in the least what your father wants if something terrible happens to him. Thus, we have more important things to worry about right now. I'd like to see that note. Can you show it to me?"

"Yes, I—" Grace didn't have time to finish her sentence, because the door near where they were standing opened to deposit her brother into their midst. Rosemary groaned internally at the interruption, thinking perhaps it hadn't been wise to attempt investigating with so many people milling about.

Theodore took a surreptitious look around as Rosemary, amused at the thought he might still be avoiding Marjorie Ainsworth, watched and wondered why.

To add insult to injury, Frederick appeared at the other end of the hall and strode with purpose in their direction. Upon his arrival, Rosemary introduced him to Theodore and Grace, repeating the ritual of politeness in which she had been forced to engage all evening.

"I don't know why our paths have never crossed, but it's a pleasure to meet you all the same." Frederick offered his hand to Theodore, who echoed the sentiment. Next, he turned to Grace and made a show of gallantly kissing her hand. "Lovely to meet you, as well."

"Likewise," Grace said, displaying none of the womanly indications of attraction that Frederick generally took for granted. He peered at her for an extra moment, and Rosemary idly wondered if her response made Grace more appealing to her brother, or less.

Teddy clapped Frederick on the back and gestured towards the ballroom. "Care to join me for a drink? I need a shield, and I believe you'll do nicely." Frederick nodded, and Teddy caught his sister's arm. With no other choice but to follow, Rosemary and Grace abandoned their escape plan, sharing a look of amused frustration as they returned to the ballroom.

Now that the trays of canapés had been emptied, the toasts lifted and lowered, the formalities observed, most of Mr. Barton's' colleagues had taken their leave. Only a smallish group of the most dedicated partygoers remained behind.

"Rosemary!" A trilling voice cut through the din of music and the sound teased from Rosemary an involuntary smile. Whirling, she found herself standing under the beaming gaze of Lorraine Blackburn. "You look absolutely ravishing, darling!" Vera's mother took Rosemary by the shoulders, held her at arm's length for a better look, then pulled her close and planted a kiss on each cheek.

As she always did, Rosemary blushed under the attention and swept her eyes over Mrs. Blackburn's dress. "Not as ravishing as you. You practically glitter," she said.

"It's been far too long, my dear, since you have visited the countryside. I must insist you and Vera spend a day with me. We'll go for a walk out to the shooting range and practice our aim. What do you say?"

Mrs. Blackburn had to be one of the few women Rosemary knew who took as much delight in target practice as she did in getting dressed for a party. Unsurprisingly, she was a crack shot, better than the vast majority of men who had tried to outdo her.

"I say yes, of course. I wouldn't dream of missing the chance to spend quality time with you and Vera. It *has* been too long, and I can't say I abhor the idea of letting off a little steam." Rosemary found as she said the words that they were very true.

Lorraine smiled her dazzling smile and gave Rosemary a wink. "It's time for me to rejoin my adoring public and regale them with naughty tales from my glorious past treading the boards. Ta-ta!" And with that, she sashayed back across the dance floor with a spring in her step that caught the attention of every eye—at least, every male eye—in the room.

The distraction served Rosemary well, as she and Grace used it as cover to slip away once more.

Chapter Eight

Grace led the way through a series of turns which Rosemary committed to memory. After all, no investigator worth their salt ought to get lost in a house. Finally, after ascending a curving staircase, Grace slowed, and her motions turned furtive as she approached a closed door about halfway down another short corridor.

"Father lets no one else in here. He'd be furious if he knew I'd invaded his privacy once already," Grace admitted, "and even more enraged to know I'm about to do it again."

Rosemary wondered what had prompted Grace to enter the forbidden room in the first place, but didn't have time to ask before she twisted the knob and threw the door open. What happened next obliterated the thought entirely.

When Grace stopped short, Rosemary rammed into her back so hard it was a wonder she kept from knocking her companion flat.

"Oof!" Rosemary exclaimed and stepped around to find Grace wide-eyed and open-mouthed in the midst of a silent scream. "What?" She reached out and gave the smaller woman's arm a shake.

When there was no response, Rosemary tracked Grace's gaze to a large desk positioned at the back of the room, surrounded by built-in shelves crowded with books and assorted bric-a-brac. Several of the drawers had been pulled open, and there were papers scattered across the surface as though someone had emptied the wastepaper bin right on top of the desk.

Shocking as the mess was, there was worse to come. A brown-haired man sat in the ostentatious leather swivel chair, his head lolling to one side. From where Rosemary stood, it appeared as though Mr. Barton had escaped from the party and retreated to his study. Which wouldn't have been scandalous except for the blood spattered across the top of the desk and the bullet hole in his temple.

Rosemary's stomach heaved as she remembered that, not too long ago, she'd been thinking about guns and had enjoyed the thought of putting holes into a target. It heaved again when she recalled how she had dubbed Lorraine Blackburn a crack shot, but pushed the thought out of her head as it had no bearing on the scene laid out in front of her.

Hadn't she seen Mr. Barton downstairs shortly before escaping the party? How could he possibly be dead in this room now? Released from her stasis and wailing with pain, Grace rushed around to the other side of the desk, and Rosemary watched as her face changed from horror filled to relieved, and then back again.

"It's not Father. It's Uncle Ernest." With that, Grace's last ounce of control broke, and she began to scream with high-pitched wails.

Pushing the shock of seeing the body aside, Rosemary sprang into action.

"Come away, now. Shh." The sounds of the party had muffled Grace's screams, but Rosemary needed her lucid, and so she gave the woman a gentle shake before leading her from the room. "I need to telephone the police."

Mind racing, Rosemary led the limp woman downstairs to make the call. Then, because Grace could only stare while her mouth worked, Rosemary informed Mr. and Mrs. Barton that there was a dead body in the study. To say the news dampened the mood of the whole anniversary celebration would be a gross understatement.

Once the police had arrived and sequestered most of the guests in the ballroom, time passed slowly. Rosemary found herself and Grace occupying one of the more secluded front rooms of the house along with the rest of the Barton family. Though Rosemary had plied her with brandy and tried to hand her off to an uncharacteristically solemn Theodore, Grace still clung to her as if she were a life raft.

After what seemed an eternity, Geoffrey, the Bartons' butler, ushered Mr. and Mrs. Woolridge, followed by Frederick and Vera, through the door.

"Are you girls all right?" Concern coloring her voice, Mrs. Woolridge went to Rosemary, scrutinizing her daughter closely.

"They're fine, Evelyn," Mr. Barton barked, "though the same can't be said for poor Ernest."

"Yes, yes, of course, Edgar," Mr. Woolridge interjected, answering for his wife. "It's a tragedy." He appeared to want to say more, but remained silent, as was his custom. He directed a searching look towards his daughter as if to evaluate her condition. His eyes met hers, and Rosemary nodded once to indicate she was, indeed, perfectly fine. As perfectly fine as one could be under such circumstances, at least.

"When we entered the room," Rosemary explained even though she hadn't been asked, "Grace thought it was you." She looked at Mr. Barton. "You see, the chair was turned just so, and all she saw was a head of similarly colored hair. She's still a bit shaken. The brandy is helping calm her nerves."

Mr. Barton's eyes widened, whether due to the actual words Rosemary had uttered or her outspokenness, she couldn't discern. "Why on earth would anyone want to murder me? And why would they do so with a whole ballroom full of guests present? Awfully risky."

"Certainly," Rosemary agreed, noting that Mr. Barton appeared incredulous although he'd recently received a death threat.

"It was risky, which means whoever did it must have been desperate. Desperate enough to move quickly, and with haste comes mistakes. Mistakes we may be able to use to track him or her down."

She realized her own mistake rather quickly as Mrs. Woolridge cut in with a sharp reprimand. "There is no "we" involved, Rosemary. You will leave this matter to the police."

Evelyn didn't add that she believed Rosemary had become too entrenched in her late husband's work, but she needn't have voiced those concerns, anyway, because Rosemary had heard them enough times to assume that was exactly what her mother was thinking.

In any case, Andrew's job had not involved the solving of murders, though no amount of explanation to that effect had changed Evelyn's view of the work. What she knew of private investigations came from the penny dreadfuls she devoured every chance she got.

Thankfully, the Bartons were so involved in their own thoughts that none, save Theodore, who peered at Rosemary with curiosity in his eyes, paid much attention to what Evelyn had said.

For that matter, neither did Rosemary herself. She'd come here to try to ease Grace's mind—had been brought here, really, to prevent a murder from happening. Only she had failed, and a murder *had* happened, even if the victim had not been the expected target. Still,

Rosemary didn't believe in coincidences, and now she was right and fully intrigued.

"I just can't believe this has happened," Mrs. Barton said, her back ramrod straight in her chair, while she wrung her fingers nervously.

It was the first time the woman had displayed anything other than contempt or irritation, and it reminded Rosemary that there was a person inside the cantankerous shell of Mrs. Barton. A woman who had thoughts and feelings, and who, despite the wealth at her disposal, did not appear to have much joy in her life.

Mr. Barton's eyes narrowed as he gazed upon his wife. "Pull yourself together, Eva. Now is the time to show fortitude." His eyes roamed to his daughter and softened slightly.

Any further discussion was cut short when the parlor door opened and in walked a man who was, to Rosemary anyway, as familiar as an old, comfortable sweater. His deep, chocolate-brown eyes met hers and widened slightly with surprise, but he maintained his composure as he made his way across the room to greet Mr. Barton.

"Hello, sir. My name is Inspector Maximilian Whittington, and I'll be handling this case." He thoroughly shook Mr. Barton's hand. "I have performed a preliminary search of the scene, and determined that time of death was around eleven forty-five—not much more than a half hour before the body was found. Most of the party had, as I have been informed, left by that point. My lads are taking statements from the guests still present. We ought to have them all dismissed within the hour. However, I'll need to ask each of you a few questions, starting with whoever was unlucky enough to have found Mr. Cuthburt's body."

Mr. Barton pointed to Rosemary and Grace. "My daughter and her friend found Ernest in the study. But poor Grace is absolutely distraught. Is it necessary to put her through the ordeal of explaining herself at this very moment?" His brusque tone rubbed Rosemary up the wrong way, and she noted the way Max bristled at his words.

"Not immediately, no, but I will need to talk to her before the night is over. For now, I'd like to talk to Rosemary. Is there a place where we can talk in private?"

Seemingly appeased, Mr. Barton directed them towards the parlor door.

"Mr. and Mrs. Woolridge, it's a pleasure to see you, though the circumstances are, once again, less than ideal," Max said, stopping on his way past Rosemary's parents and referring to the last time they had met, which had been at Andrew's funeral. Max and Andrew had been chums throughout school, and then partners in the police force before Andrew had come into his inheritance and opened Lillywhite Investigations.

After exchanging pleasantries, Rosemary and Max followed Mr. Barton to another sitting room on the opposite side of the entrance hall. Once the door had closed behind him, formality went out of the window. This was a man Rosemary knew she could trust, though whether he would accept her interference in the case was another matter entirely.

CHAPTER NINE

"What are you doing here, Max? Have you taken on a sudden yearning to settle in the country?" Of anyone she knew, Max would be the last person she might expect to leave London for the simpler life.

His laugh rolled out rich and deep. "Never. I've only come on a temporary basis while the local inspector takes a short leave of absence. It's a matter of sheer luck to run into you in such an unlikely place."

Sobering, Max dipped his head. "How have you been getting along, Rose?"

Eyes boring into hers as if to discern whether she offered complete honesty, he shifted from one foot to the other. He would have liked to take her into his arms and offer whatever comfort he could, but could not seem to command his body to cooperate with his wishes.

Rosemary sincerely wished people would stop asking her how she was doing, and if it had been anyone else, she might have given the standard, rehearsed answer. But this was Max, and so she told the truth.

"In some ways, I'm feeling a bit better. In others, a bit worse. I think that's just how these things work, don't you?"

Max nodded in agreement. "Yes, I believe you've hit the nail directly on the head, as usual." He sat down on one of the sofas and Rosemary followed suit. "Now, tell me why you're here and exactly what happened. All the details you can remember, you never know—"

"What might be important. Yes, I understand how these things work," Rosemary cut in wryly. "I may as well start at the beginning." She explained yet again how Grace had found the death threat in Mr. Barton's study, but did not divulge that Grace had been seeking out Andrew in his professional capacity when she'd arrived at Rosemary's townhouse. It was true she had known Grace from school, and allowing Max to believe she had merely been helping out a friend was a lot less dangerous than letting him know she'd intended to play the role of sleuth.

"I couldn't turn down someone in such need, and so I enlisted Vera's help, and traveled to Pardington to see if there was any merit in Grace's concerns. You would have been my first call if I had discovered any solid evidence. But then, we found Mr. Cuthburt—" Rosemary realized she'd been rambling and cut herself short.

"That's a fascinating story, Rose, and though I wish you had called upon me immediately, I'm glad you were at the scene. At least I know I'll get one truthful account of the goings-on here. Please, continue." Max looked as though he wanted to say more, but continued jotting things down in the little notebook he'd pulled from his breast pocket.

To cover a moment of chagrin over offering a mildly deceptive story, Rosemary stood, crossed the room to the drinks trolley in the corner, and poured herself a brandy. "Would you like something?" she asked, feeling no remorse for helping herself, considering the circumstances.

Max shook his head. "On duty."

"Of course."

Sticking to the salient points, Rosemary launched into her recital.

"Vera and I arrived at about eight thirty. The victim—Mr. Cuthburt—exited from a room leading into the entrance hall. He and the butler, Geoffrey, exchanged words, and then we were ushered into the ballroom. Grace introduced us to several people, including Mr. and Mrs. Barton. I can't say Mr. Barton made the most favorable impression on me, and just between the two of us, the possibility of him having enemies came as no shock after meeting him."

Allowing her disdain for the man to show did not mean she wished him to die.

While he continued to take notes, she told Max about the people she had met: Mrs. Barton, who held the unenviable title of wife to Grace's father; Arthur Abbot, who had been an insufferable bore, but overall quite jolly; the beautiful and enigmatic Marjorie Ainsworth, with her sights set on Teddy and then Frederick; and finally, Herbert Lock—a man who Rosemary confessed she disliked even more than Mr. Barton.

"There was violence in him, Max. Truly, there is another side to that simpering excuse for a man. One who would not hesitate to lay his hands on Grace, or any other woman, I assume. Unfortunately, he also wanted Mr. Barton's money, and as far as I'm concerned, that puts him out of the running as a viable suspect." Rosemary had to admit it would be nice and tidy if Herbert Lock were the murderer, but she couldn't see him killing the fatted calf.

Max raised an eyebrow. "Explain your reasoning, won't you?"

"Obviously, him killing Mr. Barton would put paid to his plans entirely. Anyone with eyes can see Grace doesn't want to marry Herbert, but she would out of a sense of duty to her father."

Lifting the glass, Rosemary let another sip of the smooth brandy slide down and warm her insides.

"Only after the marriage, perhaps, would it have been beneficial to have Mr. Barton out of the picture, but not before. Granted, I do not take Herbert for the most intelligent chap, but he's been duplicitous enough to convince Mr. Barton to consider letting him marry his daughter when more suitable men have vied for the privilege, so he must have more than just fluff between his ears."

A frown marred his brow as Max considered all the information Rosemary had given him.

"All this and you've only been in the house for a matter of hours." He shook his head, but a small grin played across his lips. "I can't say I like the idea of you being involved in a murder, but you do have a knack for ferreting out the deepest and darkest secrets."

After Andrew had given up his post as inspector, he had regaled Max with tales from private practice, many of them centered around Rosemary's deductive skills. Looking at his notes, Max concluded Andrew had not exaggerated when he'd extolled the virtues of his wife.

Rosemary dismissed the praise. "It's merely a matter of being observant."

Shrewd as she might be, Max's conscience would not allow the wife of a good friend to stand in the path of danger.

"Rosemary, I appreciate your insights into the matter, but I have to ask you to take a step back and let me handle the case from here on in."

When she merely raised an eyebrow, Max continued, "You were at the scene of the crime, as were several members of your family. My job will require me to question everyone, and until I can clear them from the suspect pool, they will be under investigation the same as everyone else involved."

He cleared his throat and offered an apology. "Despite our personal connection, or rather because of it, I can't be seen to play favorites."

"Nor would I expect you to." Rosemary allowed the slightest chill to enter her tone. "Do your worst; my family will stand the test."

The breadth and depth of Max's feelings towards her, should Rosemary have been allowed to know them, would have shocked her senseless. Bringing up the matter felt too much like picking at an open wound, and he would rather reach his bare hands into a pot of boiling water than cause her any more pain than she had already endured.

"Max," Rosemary said, mimicking his earlier tone, "I appreciate your concern, but I am already involved, and if you think for one second I have any intention of walking away from this case while my family is under scrutiny, you are sorely mistaken. Now, I still have the rest of my official statement to give, so I suggest we adjourn to the scene of the murder where I will show you exactly how we found the body."

As far as Max was concerned, the conversation was far from over, but he clamped his jaw shut and followed Rosemary to the door without another word.

Chapter Ten

Rosemary wanted to squirm under Max's gaze as she led him to the room where, less than an hour earlier, she had found a dead body.

"You needn't stare at me as though I'm made of glass and you're expecting me to break at any moment." Amusement seemed inappropriate given the circumstances in which she found herself, but really, the man was the living limit. "I promise not to succumb to a case of the vapors or fall into a faint at your feet."

While not previously so intimately acquainted with death as on this occasion, Rosemary had dealt with the harsh realities before. Looking down at the slumped body, she felt both saddened and sympathetic at the evidence of a life cut short. She allowed those feelings to guide her through the unpleasant task of revisiting the crime scene, knowing that the images would remain etched in her memory for years to come.

"Give us a few moments, Officer Stalwart," Max instructed the constable stationed inside the door as he poked his head into the study, "but stay close. Nobody gets in here without my express permission."

The aptly named Officer Stalwart, with his thick, rope-like arms, appeared as though he'd enjoy nothing more than to be called upon for a task involving necessary force. He nodded once and positioned himself on the other side of the door with a formidable expression on his face lest anyone unauthorized for entry attempted to gain access.

Rosemary entered the room just as she had before. "Grace was the first to walk inside. She stood just there, and when she stopped short, I came up hard against her back. It wasn't until I came around and saw the expression of sheer horror on her face that I knew something terrible had happened."

She repeated her steps from before.

"Mr. Cuthburt sat slumped over in the chair, although based on his hair color, and due to the angle, for a moment we thought it was Mr. Barton who had been shot." Rosemary retraced her steps and came to stand in front of the body. "We approached and realized our mistake. It was clear that Mr. Cuthburt was deceased, so I refrained from touching the body at all. I can vouch for Grace as well."

"Is that all?" Max asked, his face a mask and his tone light. Rosemary recognized the tactic, as it had been one Andrew frequently employed.

She looked him square in the eyes and replied, "Yes, that's all. We touched nothing save the doorknob on our way in and again on our way out."

Max appeared to accept her answer for the truth it was and allowed his shoulders to relax slightly. "All right then. Now, I need you to tell me if anything here looks any different than it did when you found the body."

Rosemary appraised the area behind the desk within a matter of seconds, the mental photograph she had taken earlier still swimming vividly behind her cornflower-blue eyes.

The jumble of papers, the empty bin, the spatter of blood. Everything looked the same.

"Nothing has been touched or, if it has, everything has been set back to exactly where it was before. Do you suspect that the scene has been tampered with?"

"I suspect that something—besides the obviously dead man—is amiss. Before I allowed anyone to examine the area, I thought it best to eliminate the possibility that someone contaminated the scene *after* you and Grace had found the body."

Understanding, Rosemary nodded. "You wanted to determine whether it was the murderer—or perhaps Mr. Cuthburt himself—who rifled through the contents of Mr. Barton's desk."

The conclusion seemed more than obvious to Rosemary, and she was getting a bit frustrated with Max's continued attempts to test her mettle—and her intelligence. She had always felt respected by her husband's former mate, and now she wondered if she had been mistaken. Still, Rosemary called upon a deep reservoir of patience and maintained her composure.

She did, however, allow a few choice words to roll through her head while Max assessed her further.

"Yes, that is exactly what I would like to discern," Max replied evenly. "Along with the current whereabouts of the letter Grace described. You never actually saw the letter, did you?" he asked.

"No, but Grace indicated it was in one of the desk drawers. After we found the body, all thought of looking for it went straight out of the window."

Max's brow furrowed, and he pulled a pair of gloves out of the depths of his jacket pocket, put them on, and began carefully searching through each of the desk drawers. "Now, technically, you ought not to be present for this search, Rosemary, so I have to ask for your full cooperation and discretion," Max warned. "Not that I expect any less," he rushed to say after her composure finally broke and she directed a scathing glare in his direction.

This Max and the one with whom she'd spoken upon his arrival seemed two sides of a coin. This Max was all business.

He hadn't wanted to anger her, not really, and he respected that she could remain calm even while observing the worst of what one human being could do to another. But he also found Rosemary interesting when she was right and fully riled up.

Max continued his search and finally returned each of the drawers to their original positions. "Whatever was here," he said, "is here no longer. Which means either Grace was mistaken, though that seems unlikely, or the letter was indeed removed. I'll need to talk to Mr. and Mrs. Barton, as well as Grace, to see if someone moved it before the party. It's also possible the letter has nothing at all to do with the murder and is simply a coincidence."

The expression on his face told Rosemary he didn't really believe that, and it made her feel better to know he would continue to investigate every lead there was to follow.

"I suppose there's no way to keep Grace out of it," Rosemary mused. "Mr. Barton is still unaware she found that letter, and I don't believe she needs to endure any more stress right now. He will be angry, I am sure, despite the gravity of the situation."

"I'll do my best," Max promised. "But understand that everyone who attended the party, including Grace, is still under suspicion.

Anyone present at the time could have followed Mr. Cuthburt up the stairs and shot him before he had a chance to defend himself."

"It could just as easily have been a woman, is what you are implying. You are correct in that, Max. What I'd like to know is what the man was doing sitting in Mr. Barton's chair. The last time I saw him, he was toasting the happy couple. Like I told you downstairs, I wasn't paying much attention after that, and my eyes were mostly on Mr. Barton, considering he was the one I thought to be in danger. Also, the two men wore nearly identical suits, which made identifying their movements even more difficult."

Rosemary was regretting having come to Barton Manor at all. If Max harbored similar thoughts, he wisely kept them to himself.

"I will take it from here, Rosemary. We don't know if the murderer was aiming for Mr. Cuthburt or Mr. Barton, and regardless, he or she is still out there. If Mr. Barton was indeed the intended victim, and Cuthburt's death was a mistake, the murderer could strike again. I don't want you getting caught in the crossfire."

Rosemary steadied herself with a deep breath and then said with a mischievous glint in her eye, "If I'm a suspect, I assume I am expected to not leave the area. That *is* what you said, isn't it? That *everyone* at the party is a suspect and will need to answer questions. My family lives a few miles away, and I have just decided that a little time at Woolridge House is exactly what the doctor ordered. I appreciate your concern, Max, but I will stand with my family until all of them are cleared."

"No one is above suspicion, Rosemary. You know that. Your family attended this party, which means they're connected to the Bartons at the least. I'll do my best, as I said before, but I can't let personal relationships stand in the way of this investigation." Max's eyes searched Rosemary's face, his own a blank mask. He'd landed in an unenviable situation, and now he was stuck between duty and friendship.

She softened, realizing the conundrum he was in, held his gaze, and nodded once to let him know she understood.

Rosemary would have liked to have left Max overseeing the processing of the crime scene and taken the opportunity to meander through Barton Manor on her way back to the drawing room where her family, Vera, and the Bartons were waiting, but he insisted on walking her downstairs.

"Wait here while I have a word with my officers," Max commanded, leaving Rosemary in the hallway where she had stood at the start of the night. Her gaze turned towards the door from which she had seen the now-deceased Mr. Cuthburt duck out shortly after her arrival.

She peeked into the open door of the ballroom and noted that most of the guests had been sent on their way, their statements recorded and logged.

Along with a handful of the village residents, Marjorie and Herbert were still present, as was Mr. Abbot and his doctor, and Mrs. Blackburn's unmistakable voice drifted to her as well. Vera would be inside and chomping at the bit to hear every tiny detail, but she would have to wait.

Rosemary knew Max would go over each statement with a fine-tooth comb and wondered what sort of secrets and lies he would uncover.

No matter, she thought to herself; *I have my own ways of obtaining information, and they're far more entertaining than sitting behind a desk reading only the bits people want one to know.*

Max was standing in a group with two other officers, but he kept one eye on Rosemary, giving her no choice but to leave her exploration of the mystery door for another time. A moment later, he was at her side again, leading her back to the front of the house.

CHAPTER ELEVEN

During their absence, Mr. Barton appeared to have consumed several more glasses of whisky, enough that he tottered when Rosemary and Max reentered the drawing room.

"What is the meaning of this?" he blustered. "How dare you keep us cooped up in here? I will be speaking to your superiors about the conduct of their employees, I can promise you that. None of us left the ballroom all night if what you are trying to imply is that it was a Barton who committed this crime. Ernest is—was—my dear friend and a valued business associate. By Jove, he was the children's godfather! I demand you take your leave and allow my family to get some much-needed rest."

His eyes drooped, his speech was slurred, and Rosemary had to once again call upon her patience to keep herself quiet. Having searched the ballroom for, and been unable to locate, Mr. Barton on at least one occasion, she knew his alibi for a falsehood. Not to mention those he had tried to provide the rest of the family.

After his run-in with Marjorie Ainsworth, Teddy had retreated to who-knew-where. For that matter, Grace herself had been absent for a portion of the evening both during and prior to the altercation with Herbert Lock.

An unpleasant thought occurred to Rosemary, and her gaze swept across the room to Grace, whose face still carried the haunted expression it had worn since they had found the body. Rosemary leaned a little closer to Vera, who stood at her elbow and placed a comforting hand on her friend's back, watching avidly while Max's jaw clenched in frustration.

As expected, Vera nearly vibrated with suppressed emotions.

"Mr. Barton, sir, I know this situation is difficult for you and your family, but your safety is my number one priority—" He had not the chance to say anything more, because at that moment the door burst open and in walked Lorraine Blackburn, looking none the worse for wear after the events of the evening. Her cherry-red lipstick wasn't even a little smudged, not one blond hair out of place.

She paused in the doorway as if the assemblage of people in the room had gathered expressly for her arrival, and Rosemary was sure the pose she struck had been rehearsed in front of the many mirrors lining the walls of the Blackburn house.

"Vera, my love, there you are. The very handsome gentlemen in uniform refused to let me leave the ballroom. They kept us all caged in as if we were animals. Considering the circumstances, one cannot blame them for their caution; however, I hardly think I'm a viable suspect and would have rather been allowed to check on my daughter."

Lorraine's gaze caught the sharp look Max had thrown her way when she mentioned his men, and she threw her head back in inappropriate laughter. "I didn't mean to offend, Inspector...?"

"Inspector Whittington. I don't believe I've had the pleasure," he said, holding out his hand for hers as manners dictated he must.

"Lorraine Blackburn, and the pleasure is all mine," she purred, prompting Vera to stiffen slightly. No matter how many such displays Vera was exposed to, Rosemary knew her friend never ceased to be amazed at Lorraine's need to be the center of attention.

Casting a glance at Evelyn, Rosemary felt thankful for the grace her own mother showed under pressure.

"She's got nerve, your mother," Rosemary whispered to Vera. "It's no wonder where you get it from."

"Shut up, Rosie," Vera whispered back, but there was a note of amusement in her voice that let Rosemary know she was more embarrassed than angry, and resigned nonetheless.

"Evelyn dear," Lorraine turned and focused her attention on her dear friend, giving Max a full view of her rather spectacular rear end as she turned her back on him. It had been said by many an admiring man that the ravages of time had had little luck depleting Lorraine's good looks, and the assessment was a fair one.

The overused compliment often followed the sentiment that she and her daughter looked more like sisters than mother and daughter. "Haven't they already grilled you to within an inch of your life? Why on earth have you not been allowed to return home? Or are you simply soaking in the intrigue and enjoying yourself as I am?"

While Rosemary adored Lorraine, if primarily for having bestowed Vera upon the planet, she refused to distort her view of the woman through rose-colored lenses. Putting Evelyn on the spot like that was something Lorraine did far too often, and now was not the time for such behavior.

If Rosemary hadn't known for certain there was a loving heart beneath Lorraine's shenanigans, she would have thought the woman enjoyed leaving chaos in her wake.

Having finally had enough, Mr. Woolridge cleared his throat loudly. "We are truly sorry for what happened here tonight, but how much longer are we expected to wait? You have spoken to my daughter and my wife, and I will answer any questions you have, but I implore you to ask them quickly as it is getting rather late." Unlike Mr. Barton, Rosemary's father's demeanor held no antagonism, and his tone was respectful.

"Yes, sir, I understand." Max handled the whole scene with the blank look of someone who had experienced far worse, surrounded by considerably more deplorable company. "Miss Blackburn, has your statement been taken?" he asked Vera.

She confirmed that it had and Max nodded. "I understand you and Rosemary arrived together. You are free to leave. I will interview Mr. and Mrs. Woolridge and send them on their way. I'm afraid, Mr. Barton, that you and your family will be availed of my company a while longer." Rosemary didn't think him the least bit remorseful and took a small amount of pleasure that Mr. Barton was getting back some of the attitude he fully deserved.

"Thank you, Max," Rosemary said for both herself and Vera. "Mother, Father, I'll see you at home after I drop Vera off. Lorraine, would you like to come with us?" She had an ulterior motive but kept her face innocent.

"Yes, Mother, why don't you come with us?" Vera insisted. "But I think I will stay with Rosie tonight if Mr. and Mrs. Woolridge don't mind." The decision came as a surprise to Rosemary, but a pleasant one. She would feel safer with Vera in her bed, even if her friend did tend to hog the covers.

Evelyn wouldn't have dared refuse Vera right in front of Lorraine, though Rosemary had to admit she would not have done so under the circumstances, regardless. "Of course, dear. You three go on ahead. Your father and I will be along shortly."

Rosemary cast a glance at Max after bidding goodbye to the Bartons and whispering in Grace's ear that she would call on her in the morning.

"I would walk you out," Max said apologetically, "but I need to wrap this up. There's a constable by the front door. Ensure that he sees you to your car."

Promising to do just that, the three women made their way to the exit, Lorraine appearing slightly disappointed she was unable to stay around and eavesdrop.

"Wait just a moment, please," Teddy Barton said, having extricated himself from Grace's grasp. "I'd be happy to walk the ladies to their car unless you consider me a possible fugitive should I leave your sight." He peered at Max as if for approval. The inspector glanced between Teddy and Rosemary as though he might protest, finally resigning himself and nodding in agreement.

Teddy escorted the women outside, taking the opportunity to talk with Rosemary while the driver helped Vera and Mrs. Blackburn into the car. "You're taking this whole thing in your stride," he said, a note of admiration in his voice. "Most women would be reduced to a puddle of tears like my dear sister, but you appear unruffled. Why is that?"

Rosemary bristled slightly at his comment. She had hoped Teddy Barton was more evolved than his father, but perhaps he also enjoyed subjugating women. "I have seen men who can't handle the sight of blood or look a dead body in the face. Becoming unnerved at the realities of death is not an exclusively female trait," Rosemary retorted. "Thank you for your concern, but I really ought to be getting home now."

"Wait just a moment. I didn't mean to offend you." Teddy realized he had put his foot firmly in his mouth and rushed to defend himself.

"Perhaps not, but the fact remains." Rosemary crossed her arms and peered at Teddy defiantly.

He appeared as though at a loss for words, and that was not something that happened to the enigmatic Theodore Barton often. The woman standing before him was a spitfire indeed. She heated his blood in a way the compliant women his father constantly threw into his path never would.

"I apologize, truly. My attempt at a compliment was inexcusably inept. You surprise me with your composure, and I'm intrigued as to how you came to be that way." Teddy appeared contrite, and Rosemary softened somewhat.

"You are forgiven. I'm probably being sensitive," she allowed. "I may not appear as though ruffled, but I find no enjoyment in this situation."

Teddy nodded towards the car. "No, I didn't mean to imply that you did. Truly. I'm sure you would like to get on your way, try to get a good night's sleep. I—I hope to see you again, Rosemary Lillywhite." He stuttered slightly, giving the impression he might have been intending to say something else, but Rosemary did not have the patience or the energy to linger upon what it might have been.

"Good night," Rosemary answered, folding herself into the back seat of the car. Vera stared at her with a thousand questions in her eyes, but Rosemary shook her head and mouthed the word *later*. She would be expected to repeat the events of the evening, including every single word of her conversation with Teddy several times to placate Vera, but that could wait.

"What a night!" Lorraine exclaimed. "Who would have thought an evening with those two insufferable bores could prove more exciting than a night on the town." She appeared positively gleeful.

Vera turned a sharp look in her mother's direction, "You're acting callously, and it's rather unbecoming, Mother," she said, her tone just as razor-edged.

"Oh, Vera, don't be such a wet blanket. Obviously, I feel sorry for the miserable sod. However, I find it far easier to handle unpleasantness with humor than despair. It keeps me from getting too many frown lines or feeling the need to swallow a handful of pills. I'm sure that handsome young inspector will figure out who did the vile deed, and then we can all rest easy knowing the murderer is behind bars."

Somehow, Rosemary doubted the Bartons or Mr. Cuthburt's family would rest easy that night. That someone had snuffed out a life while a whole houseful of people drank champagne and danced made her heart hurt and stiffened her resolve. She didn't care what Max

Whittington or her mother said. She would do everything she could to help solve the case, whether or not her assistance was accepted.

"Though, between the three of us," Lorraine continued, "I must admit I didn't care much for Ernest Cuthburt. It will be interesting to see what becomes of Barton & Co. when old Edgar is left with that surly widower Arthur Abbot as the only one to advise him," she said with a wink.

Vera's gaze whipped to her mother. "And what is that supposed to mean?" she asked.

"Nothing whatsoever, dear. Just that you can't teach an old dog new tricks. That's all."

CHAPTER TWELVE

The car pulled up in front of the Blackburn estate house, and Lorraine waited until the driver opened the door before turning to Rosemary and Vera with a glint in her eye. "Keep an eye on dear sweet Grace, won't you girls? She's been in such a fragile state, and I expect this might just push her over the edge." She leaned in to give both girls a quick peck on their cheeks, and then she was gone with a whoosh of scent and a swirl of her gown.

Vera sunk down in the seat and heaved a sigh. "That woman will drive me mad one of these days," she said, miserably. "Just you wait and see."

"It doesn't seem like too many people think highly of Grace. Or any of the Bartons, for that matter," Rosemary said thoughtfully. Vera's comment about her mother went ignored, Rosemary having heard the diatribe enough times she could recite it right along with her friend.

"Don't you think it rather odd, this whole situation? Grace coming to look for Andrew, but finding me, whose family lives just down the road? I can't imagine what the end game would be, and I definitely did not get the feeling of 'crazed murderer' from Grace, but still…"

"Personally, I have my eye on that Marjorie Ainsworth woman. It completely slipped my mind until just now, Rosie, but I saw her and Mr. Barton in a rather um, awkward situation." Vera's right eyebrow raised as she said the words 'awkward situation,' and Rosemary's jaw dropped.

"Do you mean what I think you mean?" she asked.

Vera shrugged. "I'm not entirely sure, but I saw him follow her out onto the balcony—let's see, it must have been just before my conversation with Mr. Abbot—and I decided to do some sleuthing. There's a lovely spot between the curtains where you can look through

60

the glass and also remain hidden from the view of everyone inside the ballroom and anyone out on the balcony," she explained.

Rosemary wasn't surprised her friend had managed to catch a glimpse of something scandalous, or even semi-scandalous—Vera was trained as an actress, after all, and keen observation was one of the skills she had honed to a fine point.

"Anyway, I couldn't hear what they were saying, but they had their heads together and were speaking furtively. Marjorie seemed to get upset, said something that made Mr. Barton's head look like it might explode, and then stalked off," Vera finished, her eyes bright. "If it didn't have to do with anything of an untoward nature, I will happily eat my shoe."

"I will hold you to that, my love," Rosemary said, the determination in her eyes belying her light tone. Vera must have seen Mr. Barton not long before she herself had seen him reenter the ballroom from the balcony. At least the look of irritation on his face made more sense now. Rosemary thought about it all the way back home and made a mental note to investigate the line of inquiry further at the first opportunity.

Woolridge House was quiet as a mouse when Rosemary and Vera entered, but all the same, Wadsworth stepped into the light of the entrance hall and appraised the pair with a narrow-eyed expression. "Is everything alright, madam? It's later than you'd intended."

"Yes, Wadsworth, it is. There was some excitement at the party," Rosemary replied evenly. "A man was killed." She enjoyed dropping the information and watching Wadsworth digest it. She offered no additional details but instead inquired as to the whereabouts of her maid, Anna.

"I gave her permission to retire for the evening. She has attended to your rooms, and your fire has been lit. Will Miss Blackburn be joining you?" Wadsworth asked, having adequately composed himself.

"She will. Now, stop fussing and go to bed yourself," Rosemary commanded gently. Wadsworth raised an eyebrow but said nothing except the expected 'Yes, madam,' though Rosemary doubted he would get a wink of sleep for worrying about her safety.

The fire had reduced itself to coals, and Vera pushed Rosemary towards the bath, urging her to wash and dress for bed while she tended it. By the time Rosemary had removed her makeup and changed into her nightgown, the fire was back to roaring, and she took a minute to warm herself before hunting down the pad of paper and the pencils she had packed into her case.

"Vera," Rosemary said, her eyes filled with apologies, "I'm sorry you were dragged into this. Truly, I didn't think."

Vera brushed off Rosemary's concerns. "I knew exactly what I was getting into, Rosie dear. And if you think for one second I would have allowed you to walk into this situation alone, you don't know just how much you mean to me." Before Rosemary could say another word, Vera kissed her on the cheek and retreated into the other room.

While Vera took her turn bathing, Rosemary began to sketch. It helped clear her mind, and she also wanted to ensure that she retained as many details of the crime scene as possible. as her pencil worked across the page, she bit her lip and thought about all the events that had happened that evening.

It had been odd, the way the now deceased Mr. Cuthburt had been sneaking around, and even more curious that he'd ended up in Mr. Barton's study. If he had had nefarious intentions, his meddling might have been precisely what got him killed.

Mrs. Blackburn's opinion of Mr. Cuthburt only confused matters; Lorraine was the type of woman to hold a grudge over even an imagined slight, and so she had to take Vera's mother's ire towards the man with a pinch of salt. Rosemary wished she had noticed more of Mr. Cuthburt's movements, but her eyes had been trained on Mr. Barton and anyone who appeared to harbor ill intent towards *him*.

Unfortunately, his overall attitude and demeanor were such that there might be any number of people who could want Mr. Barton dead. His wife, for example—spending thirty years married to a man who had enough ambition to aspire to great wealth, likely at the expense of his family's happiness, could drive even the most timid woman to lash out. And Eva Barton was no wallflower, of that Rosemary was sure.

Grace's father had posed a threat to her freedom. If he really had intended her to marry Herbert Lock, it would have given Grace enough ammunition to consider finding a way out no matter what the cost. Rosemary knew there was more to that story and fully intended to discover the truth, but she still could not find a plausible explanation for why Grace would have employed her assistance if she had intended to commit the murder herself. Unless she was an even more gifted actress than Vera, Rosemary was positive Grace had not expected to stumble across a body when she had entered the study.

Marjorie Ainsworth's expression during Mr. Cuthburt's toast had spoken volumes—about what though, Rosemary couldn't say. Whether it had to do with the Bartons or Ernest himself was something that bore investigating. What Rosemary knew was that Marjorie had said something to anger Mr. Barton during the evening, leaving her to assume there was a connection between the two that would need ferreting out. She wouldn't put anything past the insufferable woman.

Theodore Barton likely did not need the money his father might have left him; however, Rosemary had no idea what was the nature of their relationship. She thought about the way Frederick and their own father interacted, but knew that even with friction, there was no way her brother would resort to something as deplorable as murder.

"Oh!" Rosemary exclaimed, dropping the sheaf of sketches she had completed onto the floor.

Vera poked her head out of the bathroom door. "Are you all right, Rosie?" she asked, her face full of concern.

"Where did Freddie get off to tonight? Did you see him in the ballroom after he went off with Teddy?" Rosemary asked, pacing the room.

Vera smiled. "I don't think you need to worry about Frederick, my love. He thought it would be a good idea to place a bet with Herbert Lock to determine which idiot could consume the most gin without becoming ill. Unfortunately, I'm almost certain old Herbie slipped the barman half the pot in exchange for only filling his glass with water every other round. The last time I saw Frederick, he was half-seas over, lurching towards the bathroom. My best guess is he's passed out somewhere, sleeping it off."

"So much for brotherly love and all that." Rosemary frowned, remembering Frederick's vow to help her keep an eye on Mr. Barton. "I hope he wakes up with a hammer in his head," she said, calming down and shaking her head at her brother's questionable decision-making skills.

The sketches forgotten, Rosemary snuggled into bed and allowed the soft sounds of Vera's breathing to calm her enough for sleep. It did not come easily, but it came eventually, and the last thing Rosemary remembered thinking before she drifted off was that she hoped for a dreamless night.

Chapter Thirteen

Rosemary woke the next morning and scowled at Vera, who was lying next to her wrapped up in a cocoon of blankets and snoring soundly. The scowl quickly changed to a look of adoration when she noted the peaceful expression on her friend's face. No nightmares had intruded upon Rosemary's slumber, and she knew she could thank Vera's comforting presence for that.

By the time she had bathed and donned a charcoal-gray calf-skimming dress that still paid homage to her heavy heart yet did not make her appear as drawn as pure black, Vera was awake and her hair tamed into submission. Anna had come in to stoke the fire and eyed her mistress with concern.

"I'm perfectly fine, Anna. We both are," she added when Anna looked over at Vera with the same question in her eyes. "I promise. Please, try not to worry."

"Yes, miss," Anna murmured, though with a reluctance that suggested she could not completely wipe the concern from her mind. Poor Anna possessed a timid nature, and any change in routine tended to turn her pale with worry.

"I'm absolutely famished after our adventures last night. What are the chances there's a pile of bacon waiting for us downstairs?" Vera asked, her eyes alight with more than hunger.

Her mouth watering at the sheer thought, Rosemary's stomach grumbled. "Pretty good, I'd say. But why don't we go and find out if I've underestimated the cook?"

It might have been any other day at Woolridge House; the entire family was gathered save Frederick, including Stella and her husband, Leonard, and of course little Nelly. Rosemary rolled her eyes, a plan to find and wake her brother from his hungover stupor with a cup of cold water already forming. The folds of a newspaper hid Mr. Woolridge's face, but Mrs. Woolridge kept the conversation going for the entire group.

"Really, dear, four pieces of bacon at breakfast? Is there something you and Leonard are keeping from us, or do you have a deeply seated desire to expand your waistline for no good reason?" Evelyn prodded Stella, whose ears turned a bright shade of red when she noticed Rosemary and Vera standing in the doorway.

"Well, come on in and eat, then, Rosemary, Vera," Mrs. Woolridge continued without taking a breath. "There's tea of course, and coffee if you would prefer, toast, bacon, eggs, and fruit. Perhaps you could put a plate of the latter in front of your sister, lest she consumes all the bacon before you even get a taste."

"Evelyn, let the poor girl alone," Mr. Woolridge said, rustling his paper as he set it and his reading glasses on the table next to his untouched plate, and casting a grin at Rosemary. Nobody else in the house dared say a scolding word to Evelyn save her and her father, and they enjoyed ribbing her on the rare occasions the three were in the same room. "She will never want to eat another rasher of bacon again, and that would indeed be a tragedy." Cecil winked at his youngest daughter and refused to meet his wife's irritated gaze.

The two Woolridge daughters exchanged a conspiratorial glance, and Vera said innocently, "I think you're positively glowing Stella dear." Her eyes narrowed, and the corner of her lip turned up. "Though how could anyone blame you, with such an adorable child and a wildly handsome husband? Why, I believe you, as they say, have it all!"

Mr. Woolridge couldn't help but grin, Stella's smile expanded, and Leonard flushed six shades of red. However, Evelyn bustled out of the dining-room door citing a need for more milk even though there were two jugs of it already on the table.

Rosemary allowed Nelly to climb onto her lap and nip a slice of melon off her plate, leaning over the table as she snuggled his blond head. "How are you, Leonard?"

"Right as rain, but the more appropriate question is, how are you? Had quite an outing last night, if I've heard correctly." Leonard raised an eyebrow and appeared intrigued by a murder having occurred so close to Woolridge House.

Evelyn returned just in time to hear what Leonard had said. "Really, is this any kind of talk to have at the breakfast table? Nelly dear, go outside and play."

"But I'm not finished with the bacon yet, and Auntie Rose said she would take me out to see the horses."

Leonard cleared his throat in a way that held no real malice but caused Nelly's eyes to widen. "Go outside like your Gran asked you to. You can feed the pony, but stay out of the stables unless there's an adult present." Nelly looked like he might argue, but thought better of it. Rosemary gave him a squeeze before he hopped off her lap.

"Would you rather discuss it over lunch, Evelyn?" Mr. Woolridge asked wryly once Nelly had tottered off. "This affair is all anyone will talk about, and our family is, at least for the time being, under scrutiny. It seems to me we all ought to be on the same page."

"Why on earth would we be under scrutiny? Obviously, this—this *murder*," Evelyn nearly whispered the word, as if she thought the culprit would hear it and come looking for his next victim, "was a random act of violence. A burglar, or a tramp, perhaps. We have no connection to this Ernest Cuthburt. Surely the police will understand that, and then we can all stop discussing such unpleasantness."

Mr. Woolridge gazed at his wife with a look of incredulity on his face. "Evelyn, don't be daft. You need to face the facts. I do business with Mr. Barton *and* Mr. Cuthburt. We were both present during the time of the murder, and our daughter discovered the body. We are not out of this situation, not by a long shot."

If Cecil Woolridge had not been one hundred percent correct, Rosemary might have had to stifle a giggle at the expression on her mother's face.

"What type of business, Cecil?" Evelyn's voice had an edge to it, and for once she threw propriety out the window. It was not her custom to question her husband, and certainly not in front of their children, but the situation had made her desperate. Even the most even-keeled person in the world could get riled up and say or do something entirely out of character under such circumstances. It was one thing Rosemary had learnt, not from Andrew or her time investigating, but as a woman of the world who paid attention to her surroundings.

He sighed. "Nothing scandalous, Evelyn, and nothing for you to worry about. My lawyers did a thorough investigation before I handed over a penny. However, Ernest could have been killed for many reasons, his business dealings notwithstanding."

Out of the corner of her eye, Rosemary noted that Vera, along with Leonard and Stella, watched as the scene played out, absently depositing bites of food and sips of tea into their mouths, despite paying absolutely no attention to their meal. She couldn't blame them, given the way her mother's face now looked—as if steam were about to pour from her ears.

Mrs. Woolridge appeared to realize suddenly that she and her husband were not alone in the room. She smoothed her dress, brushed a stray lock of graying hair from her brow, and pointed her nose in the air. "If it wasn't a burglar, then it must have been one of the Bartons. After all, the murder happened inside their home, and the party acted as a distraction. You be careful, Rosemary, and you too, Vera. I'd keep my distance from *all* the Bartons if I were you."

Rosemary instantly knew precisely to whom her mother was referring: Theodore Barton, the very man she had hoped to pair her daughter with less than twelve hours earlier. She merely nodded, tamping down her irritation as was her way. Better not to rock the boat, especially when Evelyn Woolridge was on board, and in a pique besides.

"I can't imagine being invited to a party and then finding a dead body while I was there. Was it absolutely gruesome, Rose?" Stella asked, her eyes wide. Evelyn harrumphed, but for once did not rebuke her youngest daughter.

"It wasn't as exciting as it sounds, I can tell you that. The police will have their work cut out for them. So many people spread across the whole of the house—well, it doesn't make their jobs any easier, that's for certain," Rosemary said.

Leonard tipped his teacup up and took a long sip. "And to think, I could have seen both Barton Manor and been part of a murder investigation. While I'm happy to have missed out on all the gory details, I have to say I'm disappointed to have missed my chance of a look inside that monstrosity."

"The manor house, you mean?" Vera asked, her right eyebrow raised in question.

"Yes," Leonard confirmed through a mouthful of toast. "It's a perfect example of how new money has shaped the decline of traditional architecture. These big shots pay exorbitant amounts of money to an architect who believes he's won first prize, and that this is the job that will define his career. They want all the modern conveniences, but in a traditional package, and often their demands resemble a list of wants drafted by a child. What results is fodder for those of us who are lucky enough to sit back in our leather desk chairs and critique the work of others."

Rosemary's lips turned up into an amused grin. "You wanted to go to Barton Manor because you think it's ugly?"

"Essentially, yes." Leonard winked at Rosemary and ignored the reproachful look Mrs. Woolridge cast in his direction. Mr. Woolridge grinned behind the paper he had lifted back in front of his face, and the mood lightened slightly.

That was until the doorbell rang a moment later. Inspector Max Whittington walked into the dining room with a frown on his face. Rosemary felt Vera's elbow digging into her side, and recognized that her friend must have had to bite her tongue half off keeping quiet during the previous, uncomfortable conversation with Evelyn. No doubt she would have less luck now that Max had arrived.

"Mr. and Mrs. Woolridge, I do apologize for interrupting your breakfast, but I am on a tight schedule. I must insist on having a word with you both immediately. Some additional details have come to light, and there are a few more questions that need answering. I hope I am not intruding too rudely." Max knew how to phrase a demand as though it were a polite question, Rosemary assessed.

Her father rose from his chair, brushed the crumbs from his lap, and clapped a hand to Max's outstretched one. "Of course, good sir. Let us retire to my study, upstairs. Fewer prying ears, if you know what I mean." He glanced at Rosemary, allowed the glimmer of a smile to flit across his face, and then gathered his wife and led both her and Max toward the entrance hall.

"Come on, Vera. I need your help with something. Right now," Rosemary said, tugging on her friend's arm with more force than was necessary. Served Vera right for poking her in the ribs earlier.

"Rosie!" Vera protested, a piece of toast still in her hand. "I haven't finished yet."

"Yes, you have," Rosemary insisted, dragging her through the dining-room door with Stella and Leonard staring after them in astonishment.

CHAPTER FOURTEEN

Once in the entrance hall, Vera stamped her foot. "Rosemary Esther Lillywhite, what in heaven's name has come over you?" she demanded. "You're acting certifiably insane!"

"Father just gave me a signal. I think he knows more than he's letting on because I'm getting the distinct impression he wants us to listen in on his and mother's interrogation. Well, interrogation might not be the most apt description, but you know what I mean! Follow me." Rosemary didn't have to pull Vera along anymore; the prospect quite intrigued her.

"What makes you think he wants you to eavesdrop?" Vera asked.

"Because, don't you remember when we were children, one of his favorite misquotes trotted out whenever we hid in dark corners? Something about prying ears being one of the devil's playthings. He knows he will likely remember only a quarter of what Max says, and I believe he's more aware of my crime-solving history than he has ever let on. Just call it intuition, if you must, but I want to know exactly what's being said behind that door and what's more, *how* it's being said. I may believe Max Whittington's intentions are noble, but I *have* been wrong before."

Rosemary waited a beat. "On occasion."

That said, she marched into the parlor which was situated directly below her father's study, closed the door, and grabbed a chair. "Help me move this, quickly," she implored Vera.

Once she had positioned the chair where she wanted it, Rosemary kicked off her shoes, climbed onto the seat, and reached up to slowly open the air grate that connected to a spot underneath her father's desk. Max's voice drifted down, quiet but still audible enough for the pair to hear the conversation.

"—your son, Frederick." She heard him say, and her blood ran cold as ice.

"You cannot possibly believe Frederick had anything to do with this. He barely knows the Bartons, and he doesn't have a connection with the dead man." Cecil Woolridge spoke the words Rosemary knew both he and her mother were thinking.

"I have a witness that puts him in the proximity of the crime, around the time it occurred," Max replied on a sigh. A sigh that told Rosemary he would rather be anywhere else, talking to anyone else, and she softened towards him infinitesimally.

"My personal feelings aside, I must follow through with every available lead. Please understand, Frederick is not the only suspect, and there's only circumstantial evidence against him. All that must happen now is for me to talk with your son. I promise to do my due diligence and not jump to any conclusions, as long as you all cooperate. Do you know where he is?"

Mr. Woolridge cleared his throat loudly. "We will pass the message along to Frederick, and I am sure he will contact you as soon as he's able. Is there anything else?" Rosemary couldn't imagine Max hadn't noticed that her father didn't answer his question regarding Frederick's whereabouts, but he didn't press the issue.

"Yes, actually. It's come to my attention that you invested or had an intent to invest in one of Mr. Barton's business ventures. Can you tell me anything about that?"

"Of course, of course. I laid down a small amount of money to Mr. Barton, as a show of good faith. In fact, Mr. Cuthburt was the one who convinced me Barton & Co. was a sound investment. As yet, however, I have been ill-inclined to invest further," Cecil said succinctly.

Max paused, "And may I inquire as to the reason for your caution?"

"There have been rumors that the business is not entirely on the up-and-up. As such, I felt it pertinent to weigh my options and gather more information before committing any further funds," Mr. Woolridge explained.

"Hmm, very astute of you," Max said. "One can't be too careful, especially considering recent circumstances. Keeping distance between yourself and the Bartons would serve you well at this juncture."

"So it seems," Mr. Woolridge said thoughtfully.

The sound of a chair being pushed back alerted Rosemary that the conversation was quickly coming to a close. "One more thing," Max said. "Did either of you notice anything unusual concerning Grace Barton last night at the party? Were you aware of her absence during the window of time between eleven-thirty and midnight?"

This time it was Mrs. Woolridge who answered. "I saw her step out onto the balcony after Mr. Cuthburt's speech, and reenter with Rosemary a short time later. After that, the antics of Lorraine Blackburn distracted me, and I did not notice Grace's movements. I doubt my husband will have paid much attention. His mind has a tendency to wander."

"My wife is correct. I'm afraid I was pulled into a long conversation regarding golf and then waylaid by Mr. Abbot, who waxed lyrical about his recent art acquisition for close to an hour. I managed to extricate myself when he said he needed to attend to a personal medical matter."

"All right then, Mr. and Mrs. Woolridge. Thank you for your time," Max said sincerely. Rosemary heard him walking towards the door and climbed down from the chair upon which she was perched.

Vera and Rosemary exited the parlor just as Mr. Woolridge led Max back down the stairs to the entrance hall. The knowing look her father gave her assured her she had been correct in the assumption that his intention had been for her to listen through the grate.

"If you have any more questions, please do not hesitate to return, Inspector," Mr. Woolridge said, clapping Max on the back. "The sooner you and your men can clear up this mess, the better."

"I agree, sir," Max said. He nodded to Mrs. Woolridge and waited for them to return to the dining room before turning to Rosemary. "I would like a private moment before I take my leave if you don't object."

"No objections here," Vera answered for Rosemary while she waggled her eyebrows suggestively. Fortunately, her back was to Max, and he didn't witness the gesture. "Anyway, I think I need another slice of toast. Ta-ta."

CHAPTER FIFTEEN

"You needed to speak to me?" Rosemary asked, her tone neutral as she led Max to a pair of chairs on the veranda. They settled in, and she looked at him expectantly.

Max eyed her thoughtfully and loosed a barrage of questions, all of them personal in nature. "Rosemary, I merely wanted to see if you're all right. I know you've become peripherally involved in cases in the past, but those all concerned people unknown to you. This is different. I'm being forced to investigate you, your family, and your friends. How are you faring? Were you able to get any rest?"

He recalled the time just after Andrew had passed away and remembered the red circles that had become a regular fixture around Rosemary's eyes. No, she hadn't been close to Ernest Cuthburt, but death was death no matter how you looked at it, and being involved in a murder investigation might have dredged up feelings he was afraid she might not be equipped to deal with.

It wasn't that Max believed Rosemary a wilting flower; in fact, he considered her one of the strongest women he had ever known. Still, even steel had a melting point, and strong or not, she was only human.

"Max, I appreciate your concern, but I promise you, I'm perfectly fine. Vera stayed with me, and I'm nearly positive Wadsworth ordered one of the staff to stand guard by our door all night."

Max nodded, grateful for that. "I'm afraid this is about to get even more complicated for you. The murder weapon has yet to be found, but Mr. Abbot reluctantly admitted to having seen your brother in the entrance hall, acting somewhat oddly during the window of time when the crime took place." He noted that Rosemary didn't seem surprised by the news. "Your father claims he doesn't own a gun of the caliber that was used and has assured me neither does Frederick. Abbot stressed that your brother was not carrying a weapon and that he has no reason to suspect Frederick as the murderer; however, I have to follow any and all leads to the full extent of my ability."

"You know me, and I think you respect my judgment," Rosemary replied. "I can tell you beyond a shadow of a doubt, Frederick had nothing whatsoever to do with the death of Mr. Cuthburt. Even if you can't see that for yourself, please understand that I do. I know my brother better than anyone on this earth, and he isn't capable of that level of treachery." Her nose tipped into the air as she spoke.

"I hope your faith in Frederick isn't unfounded." He waited for the onslaught of questions he thought she would ask. He might have been knocked over with a feather when instead, she offered information.

"In the interest of full disclosure, and," Rosemary raised an eyebrow, "the hopes you will continue to treat me as a friend rather than a suspect, there is something else you ought to know. Vera noticed an exchange between Mr. Barton and Marjorie Ainsworth at the party last night. I'm positive she had every intention of telling you about it herself; however, it slipped her mind during the brief questioning she received from your constable."

Rosemary explained how Vera had watched the unlikely couple exit to the balcony outside the ballroom and engage in what appeared to be an argument. "It may have nothing to do with Mr. Cuthburt's untimely death, but the possibility remains that he wasn't the intended victim and therefore Mr. Barton's actions must be reviewed. I'm sure you'll agree." Her tone indicated that if he didn't, she might think him rather daft.

"As I said, all lines of inquiry will be followed, you may rest assured. I believe I'll have a personal conversation with Miss Vera Blackburn, now that you mention it." Max's eyes took on a faraway look for a moment, and at that moment, Rosemary wondered if he found her dear friend attractive.

Of course, he does. Everyone with eyes finds Vera attractive. Max was a handsome man and a single man. Vera was a single woman. Rosemary put the image of the two of them together to the back of her mind for the time being. She had hoped her friend would find happiness again someday but had never considered her husband's former colleague a contender. Unsure what the unpleasant, niggling feeling in the pit of her stomach might be, she set her mind back to the task at hand.

75

"Please, Max, tell me where you are headed with this investigation, aside from my brother. Have you been able to narrow down the suspect pool? There were so many people milling about, not including the staff. However, it seems unlikely one of them murdered Mr. Cuthburt. I can't imagine what their motive might have been."

Rosemary allowed her eyes to well up slightly, attempting to use her feminine wiles to appeal to Max's chivalrous sensibilities. After all, he seemed to care about her well-being, and she now wondered if brushing off those concerns and citing herself as "perfectly fine" had done her a disservice.

He softened slightly, just as she hoped he would, and she vowed to be less pushy and more pleading in the future. It might not sit well with the bright young things of her time, but it was a means to an end. With her family on the line, she wasn't in the position to put pride before purpose.

"None of the staff appear viable suspects, and neither do most of the guests. The study was on the second level, as you know, and accessible via three separate routes. The servants' staircase is out, due to the fact that activity in the bowels of the house was extensive, and anyone attempting to use that means of egress would have been spotted by one of the staff."

When Max rubbed at one of his eyes, Rosemary noticed signs of fatigue. Had the poor man been up all night?

"You look exhausted, Max. Could I offer you something to eat?"

He shook his head and continued the conversation. "We already know you and Grace used the exit towards the side stairs, though your escape was noticed by the butler. That may be because he's trained to keep an eye on the members of the household, however, and it's possible someone else slipped out through that door without him noticing." Max stopped for a moment, his eyes searching back and forth even though his gaze was trained on something only visible in his imagination.

"That leaves only the main staircase, or perhaps the balcony. Is there any way the killer could have scaled the exterior wall?" Rosemary asked.

"No. There isn't so much as a trellis that reaches the second level. It's also clear from the wound that the killer was standing in the doorway."

Rosemary frowned. "The main staircase, then. Am I to assume that's where my brother was spotted?"

"Yes, and the fact that it had to be the entrance hall stairs supports the theory that the killer was someone who knows the layout of the house. By all accounts, your brother does not fall into that category, and that's why he falls low on my suspect list. I'll give him the benefit of the doubt for as long as I'm able."

In silent thanks, Rosemary laid a hand on his and kept it there for a moment.

"Woolridge & Sons has a minimal stake in Barton & Co., and Mr. Barton confirmed that until last night, to his knowledge, Frederick had never been inside the manor. The theory that Mr. Barton was the intended victim still holds water. It's almost as though I'm investigating two separate crimes. I cannot as yet discern a motive for killing Ernest Cuthburt, and I also have to be mindful that if Mr. Barton *was* the target, he might still be in danger." Max sighed and rubbed his eyes again.

"Is that why you're concerned about Grace's whereabouts?" Rosemary interjected, feeling a little like a cat pouncing on an unassuming mouse.

Max pierced her with a look. "Were you stationed outside the door with a highball glass to your ear, Rosemary? It wouldn't surprise me in the least if you were."

"Not exactly," she said evasively, "and it doesn't matter how I know. It doesn't make a lick of sense that Grace would tell me about the letter she found in Mr. Barton's desk if she intended to murder her own father."

"I agree," Max said. "Furthermore, the letter has gone missing, and if it had been part of her plan to implicate someone else, seems like she would've left it there."

"It still hasn't turned up? Did you ask Mr. Barton about it?" Rosemary inquired.

He nodded wryly. "I did not, however, alert him to the fact that his daughter was the one who informed me of its existence. I tried to lure him into telling me about the letter himself, and when he didn't rise to the bait, I cited an anonymous source and finally broke through his protests."

"And?"

"He denies receiving a letter of the type I described, which means he probably disposed of it himself."

Rosemary was quiet for a moment. "Or the murderer did. Perhaps he sent the letter, didn't get the response he wanted, and then decided to simply do away with Mr. Barton anyway. He didn't want to leave behind evidence, so he took the note with him." She threw out the first theory that came to mind and reiterated that she could not fathom Grace Barton having the temerity to kill her own father.

"I understand she's your friend, Rose, but sometimes people do things for reasons beyond our comprehension. From what I understand, she may have had a personal motive. You said yourself she has no desire to marry the man her father wants her to. Perhaps the notion of a life spent with Herbert Lock pushed her over the edge."

"Well then, I would have expected the body to have been that of Herbert Lock himself! Wouldn't that make more sense?" Rosemary retorted. "Let me help in any way I can. I was there, Max. My observations could be of some use to you, and it would ease my mind, for Frederick's sake. He *is* my only remaining brother, you know."

It was a low blow, and they both knew it, but it squarely hit the mark.

"Fine. What I have is a whole houseful of people with either a clear motive and an iron-clad alibi, or no discernible motive and no alibi at all. Mrs. Barton says she was in the kitchens, though the butler swears it was Grace who came to speak to him. There could be many personal reasons she—or either of her children—might want her husband dead. You are just as well acquainted with the type of man Mr. Barton is as I am, so that doesn't come as a surprise. Mr. Barton didn't leave the ballroom during that time, and your own parents have attested to that. Theodore Barton was in the billiard room—according to what you told me last night, avoiding Marjorie Ainsworth—and several men can vouch for him, as well as Marjorie herself. She insisted upon speaking to Theodore and according to his chums, dragged him outside like a naughty puppy. They had quite a laugh over it, from what I'm told. I didn't, however, realize Marjorie had any personal relationship with Mr. Barton, so that is a lead I will follow after I hear what Miss Blackburn has to say. Mr. Abbot was with his doctor, getting an insulin injection. The only other guest who wasn't present in the ballroom was Mrs. Blackburn, who has no discernible motive, as far as I can tell."

By the end of the speech, Max's jaw had clenched in frustration.

"This entire case is one big circle. Nobody so far has had anything bad to say about Ernest Cuthburt, and I'm at a loss for a motive that doesn't have to do with some nebulous theory about a business deal gone sour." He stood and so did Rosemary, recognizing they were nearing the end of the conversation.

Laying a hand on her arm, Max squeezed gently and delivered his request in the same way. "Please, heed my advice and stay out of harm's way. I'll need to speak to your friend briefly, and then I'll be on my way. I still have the accounts of the rest of the guests to sift through. Perhaps I'll find something that will clear Frederick, and point towards the actual killer."

Rosemary nodded. "I'll just go and get Vera for you, then. Are you certain I can't get you something to eat? I'm sure there's something left from breakfast."

"Thank you, but no. Just send Vera along."

Rosemary went and did just that, but she stayed and listened while Vera launched into a detailed explanation of her movements during the party, including the scene between Marjorie Ainsworth and Mr. Barton.

"Thank you, ladies. Your cooperation has been duly noted. I will be seeing you," Max said, nodding at each of them and then ambling down the driveway to his parked car.

Chapter Sixteen

"Well, he's quite a tall drink of water now, isn't he?" Vera said as Max passed the gate at the end of the drive.

Perhaps Rosemary had been right and the two fancied one another. She was not entirely sure how she felt about that. She had not expected Vera to be the type of woman who attracted Max's interest, though she meant no disrespect toward her friend in thinking so. Any man would be lucky to make a catch such as Vera; it was merely that Rosemary had expected Max to pursue a woman who wanted to settle into a life of family and children.

She could not have known that, deep down, a family was exactly what Vera wanted. Someday, once she had thoroughly enjoyed herself.

"I suppose he is," Rosemary agreed.

"This day is too beautiful to waste on all this drudgery," Vera said, raising her face to the warmth of the sun. "I'd far rather be at home in London, with no thoughts of murder on my mind."

"As would I," Rosemary agreed. "But, alas, here we are. And now, I can't go home until I've cleared up this mess. You, however, are under no such obligation."

Vera snorted, "Rosie, don't be daft. I've no intention of returning to London without you. We're a team; you know that."

"Vera, do you—" Rosemary didn't have time to finish her thought before Vera stood and peered across the lawn.

"Oh, look. It seems we have just found your poor hungover brother," she said, motioning toward the end of the driveway.

Frederick raised his hand in a wave, and Rosemary crossed her arms in front of herself as she watched him approach, his hair a rat's nest and his suit the same one he had been wearing the evening before.

"Where on earth have you been?" Rosemary demanded. "We thought you'd stumbled in before us at some point last night. Do you even know what's happened?" She bombarded him with questions, mimicking their mother for a moment because she knew it would irritate him.

"Lower your voice. If ever you loved me, I am begging you to have a care." Frederick pressed his thumb and forefinger against the bridge of his nose. He appeared as though he might be sick, and his sister thought it was no less than exactly what he deserved.

When silence restored him enough to ask, he said, "Has something happened?"

Rosemary let the words fall out of her mouth as though she were talking about something as inane as the weather. "I discovered a dead body in the second level study of Barton Manor."

One of Frederick's bleary eyes peered at his sister while the other dropped closed. When she repeated herself, he gave his head a shake, then winced from the pounding pain. Alternating the squint from one eye to the other, he tested Vera's face for veracity.

"And we are all suspects," Vera deadpanned. It was less than funny, but the way she delivered the line made Rosemary's lip quiver slightly.

"The inspector in charge is not the only one interested to know where you passed the nighttime hours. Tell me, where have you been, Frederick?" Rosemary demanded. "Do you have any idea how bad it looks that you've been out all night?"

Her brother looked even greener around the gills and swallowed a couple of times. "I fear I shall do my manhood a disservice and be sick if you ladies persist with this farce."

Crumpling, Frederick lowered himself to the top step, hugging his fragile middle. A shift in the breeze put the women downwind.

"Oh, my sainted aunt." Acutely uncomfortable, Rosemary fanned her hand in an attempt to dissipate the potent combination of stale tobacco and even staler alcohol. "You smell like something scraped off the floor of a dive the morning after the night before."

"Not far off the mark." Voice husky, Frederick huddled until his sister huffed out a breath.

Rising, Vera volunteered to mix up a hangover cure. Smirking, she took herself away from the fragrant wreck of a man and left Rosemary to pry what truth could be gleaned from his addled brain.

"Tell me where you've been. This is not the time to play the fool, Frederick. Not when there's been a murder, and you're a suspect."

Finally, he pulled himself together enough to look at Rosemary's deadly serious expression. "A murder? Who?"

"Grace's godfather, Mr. Cuthburt. During the party last night."

Moments passed while Frederick gathered his wits about him.

"I'm sorry, Rosie. Really, I am. But you can't believe I had anything to do with a murder, can you?"

"Of course not, you dolt. But I'm not the one you may have to convince. Tell me where you were all night."

"Well, I spent most of the evening getting sloshed with that deplorable man who Grace Barton's being forced to marry. For you, I might add, sister dear. Distracting him seemed like a better option than punching him on the nose. Which I would have thoroughly enjoyed after seeing the look on his face when Marjorie was flirting with me."

"Yes, I have heard about your little bet. But then you disappeared and have not been home since." Rosemary raised an eyebrow. "So, explain yourself. You were supposed to keep an eye on me, not that you needed to."

"Surely not, sister. That's why the second I let you out of my sight you found a dead body," he retorted.

Rosemary placed her hands on her hips and stared him down.

Sighing, Frederick acquiesced. "Fine. I popped up the bar with Teddy and then ran afoul of that horrible Herbert Lock. I've seen him a few times at the pub in town, you know, and he's always blathering on about how well he can hold his drink. I sorely wanted to find out if there was any truth to it."

"Apparently, he can hold his better than you can hold yours, brother dear." For the sake of punishment, she held back Vera's theory on how Lock had won the bet.

"Yes, Rosie, I get the point. If you must know, I spent a moderate amount of time in the downstairs loo, and the next thing I remember, I was stumbling over the gravel in the driveway. I saw Teddy on my way, with Marjorie Ainsworth in tow. Never did get that dance with her, either." His eyes took on a dreamy quality, and Rosemary nearly smacked him in the face to break him out of his reverie.

"For goodness' sake, Frederick, focus!" she yelled instead.

"Where was I? Oh yes, Marjorie was with Teddy. He didn't appear impressed, and he asked if he could give me a lift home with a look of desperation in his eyes. I declined, deciding a walk might help me sober up. This morning, I woke up beneath one of the weeping willows at the end of the lane. Are you quite satisfied? It's not one of my better stories, but it's not one of my worst, either."

"That is true. But why are you wearing that smile on your face? Did you not understand what I said? We are all under suspicion for the murder of Ernest Cuthburt! Particularly you."

"Me?" Frederick asked. "Why me?"

"Because someone saw you after you came out of the toilet. You may not remember it, but you were in the wrong place at the wrong time. Max told me Marjorie dragged Teddy outside to have a conversation with her around the time of the murder. What time was it, do you think, when you saw them?" Rosemary asked though she knew it was unlikely her brother would remember.

To her surprise, he smiled. "It was midnight on the nose. I could hear the peal of the chapel bells and thought to myself that it was far too early to have gone so far around the bend."

"Far too early, indeed," Rosemary admonished.

Frederick continued to grin, though there was the hint of a shadow behind his eyes. "Never fear, sister dear. I didn't kill Mr. Cuthburt. Therefore, I have nothing to worry about. The diligent inspector will figure it out in due time."

"So, you're not at all concerned about what Mother and Father have to say?" she fired back, ignoring the comment about Max.

At that, Frederick's face screwed up into a grimace. "I may not be out of the woods yet, after all."

Rosemary was unsurprised to get a summons from Grace Barton the next morning and fretted over what she might say to the woman while she got dressed and put on her makeup. A pale-green dress skimmed between the knee and ankle, and she had even put on a belt with a bead-encrusted buckle that Vera had insisted would match perfectly.

"Wouldn't this be the best time to wear black, though, Vera?" Rosemary asked. "Considering there was a death just the other night?"

"There'll be enough black to go around, Rosie. And you aren't mourning Ernest Cuthburt with anything more than obligation, so I think it's just fine. Besides, if we run into either of your beaus, you'll want to look your best." Vera winked and returned to the mirror where she brushed a smudge of mascara from the corner of her eye.

With a withering look, Rosemary admonished her dearest friend. "Neither of those men has any interest in me, nor I in them, and you know it."

"No, what I know is what I've seen, and what you know is nothing. You're oblivious to the fact that Max has you on the highest of pedestals, and Teddy Barton is just waiting for the right moment to sweep you out of Max's grasp." Vera eyed her friend with new eyes. "I'm right, you know absolutely nothing."

Rosemary shut her mouth and blushed six shades of red. "It matters little, regardless. I am not on the market. I'm not sure I'll ever be back on the market, Vera."

"Well, I am. This melancholy won't last forever, my love. In fact, the shadows around your face have already nearly disappeared, and the rainstorm that's hovered over your head this year has turned to a slow drizzle. Before you get defensive," Vera said as Rosemary opened her mouth to interrupt, "I'm not suggesting that you forget about Andrew. I'm suggesting that at some point, the wound won't be so fresh and you'll find that your heart has healed enough to allow room for someone else. It might be Max. It might be Teddy Barton. Or, it might be someone else entirely. I, for one, am excited to see what happens!"

"Well, I am not," Rosemary said. The mere thought of allowing another man to hold her or kiss her the way Andrew had carved a fresh hole in her misery. "And I don't want to talk about it anymore."

Vera nodded but noted that Rosemary's words didn't have quite the same conviction as they had previously had. "If you end up with Max, I'd be happy to take Teddy off your hands for an evening. He looks like a man who knows how to move a woman around the dance floor." She giggled and winked at her friend.

Not that she recognized it for what it was, but relief washed over Rosemary, knowing that Vera's sights weren't set on Max Whittington.

CHAPTER SEVENTEEN

If Rosemary had thought Barton Manor was impressive yet ostentatious under cover of darkness, it was nothing to how she felt about the place in the bright light of day. She remembered what Leonard had said about new money and even newer houses, and now, seeing walls lacking the patina of age, understood exactly what he had meant.

Wadsworth pulled into the drive and opened the door for his mistress. "I will be right here when your business concludes, madam."

"We shan't be long, Wadsworth," Rosemary promised.

Had she had her way about it, she and Vera would have met Grace at the tearoom in the village rather than go back to Barton Manor. Acting as though she were impervious to the trauma of seeing a dead body might serve her well for getting around Max, but she was, after all, only human. She wondered if she could ever forget the image of the wound to Mr. Cuthburt's head or the sickening feeling that had welled up in the pit of her stomach when she saw his lifeless body.

However, she had questions that could only be answered using her eyes and her instincts, which meant there was no other choice but to return to the scene of the crime.

Geoffrey answered the door with a clipped, "May I help you, ladies?" His expression remained neutral, as expected, but there was an impatience to his tone that implied he had other things to do and considered them more important than anything Rosemary or Vera required.

"We're here to see Grace, please. She is expecting us," Rosemary answered in a tone her mother would deem appropriate for dealing with staff, but one she was rarely forced to use when speaking to her own butler.

"Right this way, please," Geoffrey replied, leading them once again into the elegant entrance hall. "Miss Grace is out on the veranda. Straight down the hall, you will find a set of glass doors. I trust you can find your way." With a final, enigmatic look, he stalked off in the other direction.

Vera waited until he was out of earshot, then turned on her heel and returned to the entrance hall. "What an absolute pill. Did you see him putting on airs? If you hadn't given him a taste of Evelyn Woolridge, he'd have turned us out on our ears."

Mischief sparkled in Vera despite the gravity of the atmosphere.

"You really ought to be careful, darling girl, or you shall turn into your mother before you're thirty."

Rosemary tossed her head, but couldn't hold back a rueful smile. "I don't know why I put up with you, but no matter. Now is our chance to learn exactly what Mr. Cuthburt was up to during the party. He came out of that door," she said, looking around to make sure they were alone.

Curiosity mounting, the two friends crossed over to the door beneath the massive set of stairs, and Vera pushed it open. She let out a frustrated breath. Rosemary shoved past her and, to her disappointment, found herself standing in the middle of a small space that doubled as a coat cupboard and a private telephone room.

Shiny brass rods stretched across three-quarters of the coat cupboard, laden with dozens of coats Rosemary assumed belonged to the residents of Barton Manor. The narrow far wall had been stuffed to capacity, leaving an extensive section on the right-hand side empty, presumably to make room for the belongings of the party guests.

To her right rested a carved wooden desk that held a telephone, a stack of mail, and a pad and pencil for taking down messages.

"I suppose that's one mystery solved," Rosemary declared, her voice wry. "Mr. Cuthburt was merely hanging up his coat. Geoffrey is such a stickler for order and protocol; he probably didn't appreciate Mr. Cuthburt taking matters into his own hands."

Vera nodded in agreement. "I know you were hoping to find some clue here, Rosie, but I see nothing out of the ordinary. Except that Mrs. Barton owns enough fur coats to wear a different one each day of the winter. Personally, I would never relegate such fine specimens to a coat cupboard beneath the stairs. What would stop a guest from simply walking out with one?"

"I highly doubt Mrs. Barton would miss one coat from this collection. My mother would have a fit if she saw this room. She would call it a *grandiose, unnecessary display of excess*." Rosemary mimicked Evelyn's voice with such accuracy Vera couldn't hold back a giggle.

"You proved my earlier point brilliantly, though I can't argue with you. We ought to get out of here before someone notices where we have escaped to and accuses *us* of trying to make off with one of Mrs. Barton's pelts."

"Right you are," Rosemary said. "Shall we go and find Grace? Check first to make sure no one is looking."

"The key to exiting any room where one does not belong," Vera said in a lofty tone, "is simply to hold your head high, and act as if you had every right."

With that, she thrust open the door, and with her nose in the air, sailed down the hall.

But, only a moment later, Vera halted. "Do you hear that?" she asked in a stage whisper.

"No, what?" Rosemary strained to listen and heard the sounds of an argument wafting from beneath the door to one of the sitting rooms. It was the second time in as many days she had unashamedly eavesdropped, and she hoped it wasn't becoming a habit that would prove difficult to break.

"Eva, you know how hard I've been working lately. Do you honestly think I have time to cavort around behind your back?" Mr. Barton shouted. Mrs. Barton's reply was too muffled to understand, though her voice had risen to a pitch that might have cut glass.

"What do you mean, *what have I been working so hard for*? I have been trying to wrap up these business affairs, secure a few more investments, and ensure that the company is above-board. I would like to retire at some point, you know. Never have I enjoyed the company of another woman, and I will not continue being hounded about something you've made up in your head. This conversation is over!"

Rosemary and Vera hurried down the hall, eyes wide with shock and embarrassment.

"That was interesting," Rosemary commented. "But now we have to focus on Grace. Our musings on the subject will have to wait."

Chapter Eighteen

They found the object of their search curled up on a settee in the sunroom, a blanket wrapped around her and an untouched cup of tea sitting on a tray nearby.

"Grace?" Rosemary asked quietly, not wanting to startle the poor girl. Normally, Grace was a good-looking woman. A woman of great character with a quiet air about her, though on this day, she'd gone all puffy from crying. Not that anyone could blame her for such a typical response. At the sound of Rosemary's voice, Grace sat up a little straighter and motioned for her guests to take a seat.

"Please, accept my apologies for my appearance. I'm unable to dredge up the will to make myself presentable today."

Grace gave Vera's posh outfit an up-and-down look, but made no comment even though her eyes lingered over the handbag Rosemary had to admit was a statement piece if she had ever seen one. Where Vera had procured the vibrant pink-and-black patent-leather work of art, Rosemary could not begin to guess. However, what they didn't need at that moment was to make Grace feel like a wilting flower, and this was one of the few occasions when Rosemary wished her friend could be a little less fabulous.

Any irritation she might have felt evaporated—as usual—when Vera seated herself and tenderly took Grace's hand in hers. "You have nothing to apologize for, my dear, you have been through a horrific ordeal, and are more than entitled to take a day off from titivating yourself." The sincerity with which she spoke the words seeped through Grace's despair, and she allowed a small smile to play across her lips.

"Vera is right," Rosemary agreed. "We certainly didn't expect to find you in high spirits. Tell us, how are you faring?"

"I've been better," Grace admitted. "The image of Uncle Ernest just keeps swimming up behind my eyes. Sleep did not come easy, and so Mother gave me a sedative. All it did was ensure I was unable to wake from my nightmares." She shivered and pulled the blanket a little closer around her shoulders.

Rosemary was unsure what tactic to use on the poor woman. On one hand, the police were interested in Grace's relationship with her father and considered her alibi for the time of the murder as something of import. On the other, she did not seem to have any motive for harming Mr. Cuthburt and appeared an innocent victim whom Rosemary was loath to interrogate.

"Have the police been round to question you yet?" It seemed a safe enough question.

Grace's eyes narrowed. "Yes, that Inspector Whittington was here earlier this morning. He seems to think I may have killed Uncle Ernest, and that I mistook him for my father. What kind of person would do such a thing?" Either Grace was one of the most naïve young women to ever walk the earth, or she was a psychopath capable of just about anything. Rosemary's opinion leaned in one direction, but she couldn't discount the other.

"People have a way of surprising you, and it's not always pleasant," Rosemary murmured.

Grace blinked. "You believe me, don't you?" she asked.

"Of course, we do," Vera answered quickly, patting Grace's hand again. "Don't we, Rosie?"

"I can't believe you had anything to do with this, Grace. But we need to think like the police if we are going to clear you of suspicion and solve this crime. It's imperative that you be honest and transparent. Can you do that?" Rosemary pierced Grace with a look, though she felt terrible about having to do so.

"Yes, I can. What do you need to know?"

"Firstly," Rosemary began as she took a seat across from Grace and Vera, "is there anything you can tell us about Mr. Cuthburt? Anything that might be a motive to kill him?"

After a moment's thought, Grace shook her head. "Nothing I can think of. I've heard Father talk about how much he's changed since the war, and I've got the impression he wasn't always a good man. But surely that's just Father being dramatic. Uncle Ernest has always doted

90

on Teddy and me, and I can't imagine what he could have done to gain such a reputation. Surely he couldn't have been involved in anything that would have got him killed." Her voice held a heavy note of incredulity, and rosemary decided that perhaps she'd hit the nail on the head thinking of Grace as naïve.

"All right, let's focus on the theory that your father might have been the intended victim. What about the arrangement between your father and Herbert Lock? I believe the police think you may have harbored resentment towards your father for his part in attempting to pair you with that man."

"Well, I have not been pleased with father for suggesting the arrangement. I met Herbert at a dinner party my mother threw a few months ago. She knows a cousin of his, and the cousin talked Herbert up as my perfect match. From the sounds of it, he was well off and single. That's all my mother would have needed to hear. He seemed all right, at least at first. Spent more time talking to my father than he did me, and it rubbed me up the wrong way. Later he claimed he had found me so enchanting that he wanted to ensure good favor with my family, and that was why he had attempted to chum up with Father. Now, I know that to be a blatant lie, but for some reason, Father still believes him a viable suitor. As if I need my parents' help to find a husband." Grace looked like she might like to spit or say something uncomplimentary, but refrained.

Interesting, Rosemary thought, noting the slight change in Grace's tone during the last part of her diatribe. "Is there someone else in your life, Grace? Someone you would rather marry than Herbert Lock?" she said out loud.

Grace's eyes widened slightly, and her jaw wavered. "No. No, there isn't anyone else."

Rosemary caught Vera's eye, and Vera returned a wink. Grace had something to hide.

"You can tell us, you know. We promise to keep that information to ourselves." *Unless it becomes necessary to divulge it*, Rosemary added to herself. She would protect Grace for as long as possible, but if it came to light she had any part in Mr. Cuthburt's murder, Rosemary would go to Max with whatever pertinent information she had gathered.

"There is nothing to tell," Grace insisted. "But if you ask me, the police ought to focus on Herbert. He has a nasty streak a mile wide, and I wouldn't put anything past him."

"What motive could he have for killing your Uncle Ernest?" Rosemary wanted to know, and more so wanted to understand why Grace would think it.

"Perhaps he thought if he got Uncle Ernest out of the way, Father would need a new business associate," Grace speculated. "Or, maybe he was trying to get Father out of the picture, believing I might marry him in my hour of grief. Then, he would have access to any funds I might inherit."

Grace's thoughts circled the same path Rosemary's had done, but hearing Grace say them out loud shook Rosemary's confidence in the theory. It was too easy, and she didn't believe that someone like Herbert Lock would perpetrate such a crime with a flimsy motive.

She did, however, know that Grace was hiding something, and had every intention of finding out what.

"Do you know what's even more concerning? That letter I found in Father's study has disappeared. I heard him arguing with Mother about it after Inspector Whittington had taken his leave. It was the only clue as to who might have wanted to cause him harm, and it's gone." Grace sniffled. "Now, it looks as though I lied about its existence. And, to top it all off, Father knows someone was in his study before the murder, and he's furious. If he discovers it was me…"

"You aren't scared of him, are you, Grace?" Vera asked with wide eyes.

Grace grimaced. "Not in the way it sounds. I know he would never physically hurt me, but he can be quite harsh when backed into a corner. He will never trust me again, and will most likely push for my engagement to Herbert just out of spite."

"You're being rather dramatic, don't you think, Grace?" The voice of Mrs. Barton intruded upon the conversation, and Rosemary wondered how long the woman had been standing in the doorway before making her presence known. "You ought to have known better than to intrude on your father's privacy. However, I fear having Herbert Lock for a husband would be more punishment than you deserve so I will keep your secret."

Rosemary half expected Eva Barton to tell her daughter she now owed her a debt, but the woman left it at that, cast a scathing look toward the two guests, and exited the room as quietly as she had entered.

CHAPTER NINETEEN

With an audible sniff, Wadsworth eased the car to a stop on the village high street, right in front of a small tearoom. Shropshire's, he invariably pointed out, carried a scandalous reputation and ladies of Rosemary's stature and breeding ought not to frequent such establishments.

Vera, as she always did, pointed out that Mrs. Shropshire's blood ran as blue as anyone could ask, and what was the crime in opting to operate an eating establishment? It was, as both young women knew, Mrs. Shropshire's utter disdain for the bounds of society, and possibly her penchant for attending the occasional party wearing trousers in place of ladylike attire, that offended the upright soul. However, since the tearoom had become something of a fixture over the previous twenty years, she opined, it might be time for him to come down from his high horse.

This was a conversation that had been repeated many times over.

"Please return for us in two hours, Wadsworth." Rosemary let off from biting her tongue to issue the order gently. "We shall be waiting near that new dress shop on the next corner."

Vera grinned. "Make sure there is plenty of room in the boot!"

"Yes, Miss Blackburn," Wadsworth replied, his face blank but his eyes twinkling. He leaned over towards Vera, winked, and said in a low voice, "Miss, I trust you will see to it that madam buys something for herself as well."

"I have every intention of doing so," Vera said, "whether she agrees or not."

Rosemary swatted her friend on the arm. "We will shop, but first I must satisfy my craving for one of Mrs. Shropshire's famous sandwiches." Rosemary's stomach rumbled as the scent of freshly baked bread wafted through the air.

She preceded Vera inside, and, inhaling the familiar scents, recalled the many meals she had taken at the little tearoom over the years. As a testament to how long it had been since the last time, Rosemary recognized none of the workers and few of the patrons. She and Vera circled around a large pillar standing in the middle of the space, hoping to secure their favorite hidden table, only to find that a familiar face already occupied it.

"Frederick!" Rosemary exclaimed. "Shouldn't you be at the house, sleeping off your hangover beneath your bed covers or commanding Mother's staff to fetch you tea?" Thankfully, he smelled as though he'd bathed, and was no longer wearing the same wrinkled suit from the previous evening.

Her brother leaned back in his chair and grinned. "The best cure for a night of excess is a helping of Mrs. Shropshire's fish and chips. All that grease soaks up what's left of the booze."

"Frederick Woolridge, you dirty little rat! Did I hear you call my food *greasy*?" A grumpy voice caused Rosemary to spin on her heel and come face to face with the Mrs. in question.

She rushed forward to embrace the wrinkled old woman glaring at Frederick with mock indignation in her eyes. "Mrs. Shropshire, how good to see you," Rosemary said sincerely.

"If you were about to say it's been too long, you would be right, girl." An arthritic finger wagged at Rosemary. "Your rascal of a brother keeps insisting you are quite fine and that you have not, in fact, been avoiding us, but I have wondered whether he's always had brown eyes or if he's just full to the brim with cow manure. As for you, Miss Vera. If this is how frequently you visit home, you have been neglecting not only me but your dear, sweet mother as well."

Vera raised an eyebrow. "You must be the only person in Pardington who might call my mother a 'dear, sweet' anything, Mrs. Shropshire."

"You always were a disrespectful little imp. Now, come here and let me look at you." Vera preened beneath Mrs. Shropshire's gaze and did a little twirl that lifted her skirt. "Too much leg, if you ask me. Not that you would listen to the opinions of a tired old woman, anyway. Quite lovely legs, I will admit, but that does not mean you have to flaunt them in front of those of us who have only the ravages of time beneath our skirts. Downright cruel, that's what it is."

Rosemary and Vera locked eyes and giggled. The grins on their faces would have confused the casual onlooker, incongruous with the conversation as they were. Mrs. Shropshire's tongue was as sharp as the knives she used to carve her meats, and she had a history of using it to razz the young crowd. She also kept a pocket stocked with butterscotch sweets and slipped them to children when their parents weren't looking.

Once, during their disenchanted youth, Vera had drunk enough to get sloshed and then sicked up in the alley behind the tearoom. Mrs. Shropshire had found her, helped clean her up, and forced her to eat some of the aforementioned hangover-curing fish and chips. She'd let Vera off just that once, threatening to call Mrs. Blackburn if she ever so much as caught a whiff of alcohol on the girl's breath again.

Rosemary, possessed of a nature far less wild, had never required a similar threat. She had spent many an afternoon telling Mrs. Shropshire all her secrets and being doted upon in a way she rarely experienced at home. The old woman's bark was worse than her bite, and now that she had dispensed with the ribbing, the smile on her face telegraphed just how thrilled she was to have the three of them all back under her roof.

"Now, tell me, darlings, what have you come home for? Sick of London, are you? Planning on settling back into village life?"

"Actually," Frederick cut in, thoroughly enjoying himself, "Rosie and Vera are trying to solve a mystery. You've surely heard about the events last night at Barton Manor?"

Mrs. Shropshire's grin turned upside down. "Naturally. You know how fast word travels in these parts." She surveyed Rosemary, who waited for another onslaught of warnings against involving herself in a murder investigation.

Instead, the woman sat down with a grunt and pinned Rosemary with a look. "Tell me everything and don't leave out a single detail."

Unable and unwilling to argue, Rosemary gave her the short version. "Someone shot Ernest Cuthburt, and I, along with Grace Barton, found the body in Mr. Barton's study. There is some speculation regarding whether Mr. Barton himself was the intended victim, and right now poor Grace and our dear Freddie are on the inspector's list of suspects."

Mrs. Shropshire's eyebrows raised clear to her hairline. "Hogwash. Utter hogwash. Surely you don't believe Miss Grace capable of murder?" That Frederick might have been behind the caper was too ridiculous to address.

"Of course not," Rosemary replied. "There are several others who would have had the opportunity, and now we're trying to discern motives for each one. Do you happen to know anything about Marjorie Ainsworth or Herbert Lock?"

She, Vera, and Frederick leaned in while Mrs. Shropshire eased back in her chair and smiled a conspiratorial smile. "Whether it has anything to do with the murder, I couldn't say, but those two scalawags are up to no good. They have had tea together at least twice this week, and they spent the entire time huddled against one another, talking in hushed voices."

"How interesting." Vera voiced Rosemary's thoughts out loud. "Based on the conversation we witnessed between them, there was no love lost. In fact, Marjorie was pushing Herbert toward Grace, and it was clear as day she wanted Teddy for herself."

Mrs. Shropshire grimaced. "If there was a romance between them, I'll serve shoe pie for supper. Sheer greed, it looked like to me."

"Why am I not surprised that even given the hushed voices, you still managed to overhear their conversation?" Vera grinned at Mrs. Shropshire with a mixture of amusement and admiration.

The older woman winked at Vera. "Old buildings have funny echoes, my girl. 'Tisno fault of mine if voices carry to my poor, innocent ears. Mr. Lock and Miss Ainsworth spoke at length about money, and Marjorie went on at him about getting her funds back. It seems she had trusted a sum of money to Mr. Lock and had seen neither hide nor hair of a profit."

Rosemary tapped her fingers on the edge of the table while the implications chased circles in her head. If Marjorie got her hands on even a portion of Teddy's fortune, and Herbert his own on Grace's, it would set the two of them up for life.

Rosemary voiced her theory to the table. "Even so, it doesn't wash."

"What's on your mind, Rosie?" Frederick asked.

She chewed on her lip for almost a full minute before responding. "The timing is all wrong. I can't see a viable motive for killing Mr.

Cuthburt or even making an attempt on Mr. Barton. Not for that pair, anyway. Surely, they would want him alive until after the matches were final. His death would put the kibosh on the whole scheme."

"I agree." Vera nodded.

"Who else is on the suspect list, sister dear?" Frederick inquired.

"It isn't a terribly long one, according to Max. The only guests who were still present—at least, that we know of—were our family members, all of whom we can rule out, plus a handful of others. Marjorie and Herbert, the Bartons of course, and Arthur Abbot."

Mrs. Shropshire frowned. "Arthur Abbot. The name is familiar, but I can't put it to a face."

"A chronic bore about the same age as Mr. Barton and Mr. Cuthburt, I expect," Rosemary explained. "Went on and on about some piece of artwork he thought was the gnat's whistle. Unfortunately, Vera took the brunt of it."

"I certainly did." Vera shuddered and took a sip of tea. "If he hadn't been such a flat tire, I'd have thought him a poor little bunny. I expect his portion of the business has to do with keeping records or some such drudgery. Probably knows his onions, but I spent most of the time watching the large, rather disturbing mole above his left eyebrow dance around while he spoke." She shuddered again at the memory.

A wave of recognition swept across Mrs. Shropshire's face. "Ah. That one has been in here a few times. Bought a house in the village recently, from what I've gathered. Seems a decent enough chap, speaks highly of his late wife."

"Ever notice anything odd about him?" Rosemary asked. "Excepting the infamous mole?"

"Nothing leaps to mind. Came over polite and mannerly, unlike you lot of hooligans, who have kept me from my work long enough," Mrs. Shropshire said, rising with more agility than a woman her age ought to possess. "I expect I shall pay close attention the next time I see the man, and I also expect you to come around and pry for details."

Once they had piled back into the car, Frederick snorted. "My money is on Mr. Barton himself if you want to know the truth. He throws the party as a smoke screen, providing the good inspector with a plethora of suspects, and makes it look as though he were the real target. It's a brilliant plan if I do say so myself."

"You could be right, Freddie, you could be right," Rosemary mused. "Except, he never left the ballroom during the time of the murder. Perhaps it was Mrs. Barton, sick and tired of her husband turning even their wedding anniversary into an excuse to conduct business. You know we heard them arguing earlier. It seems Mrs. Barton thinks her husband is having an affair with another woman. Though, who she thinks would take a second look at that man is a mystery. Mr. Cuthburt and Mr. Abbot were both partners of Mr. Barton, he had some arrangement with Herbert Lock, and then there is the conversation Vera witnessed between him and Marjorie. It wouldn't hurt my feelings any to see that man taken down a notch or two."

Vera had listened to Rosemary and Frederick's conversation quietly. "I believe you are not alone in that opinion. We forget one vital clue, though. The letter. The mysterious letter that disappeared so very conveniently, and which may not even exist. Could Grace have misread, or is she hiding something?"

Frederick's eyebrow raised and he said thoughtfully, "If she refuses to talk with you, why not try to appeal to her brother? You know, we pay far more attention to the goings-on in our sisters' lives than we'd like them to realize. Teddy comes across as the protective type, and based on the way he was looking at you, Rosie, I think he would be more than happy to answer any questions you might be inclined to ask."

Rosemary mimicked the expression on Frederick's face, raised eyebrow and all. "I take it you do not subscribe to Mother's theory that Teddy is the most dangerous of the Bartons? Or doesn't your protective nature extend to your sister spending time with a possible patricidal maniac?"

"I have no intention of leaving you—either of you—alone with any of those people. Trust me, I have a plan."

CHAPTER TWENTY

Frederick's brilliant idea entailed inviting Teddy and Grace to the Woolridge House stables for an afternoon horse ride through the countryside. Rosemary had to admit that she'd missed the thrill of having a powerful animal beneath her, and the feel of the wind against her face as she sailed across the hills.

It seemed both Barton siblings had jumped to get away from the manor for an afternoon. Given it had only been a handful of days since the infamous party, Rosemary was glad to see the siblings bouncing back. Grace looked to be in better spirits, and Teddy also appeared more relaxed. It was an easy chore to persuade him to stick close to her side.

Welcome were the few moments of peaceful quiet as Frederick and Vera, who could have easily kept up with Rosemary and Teddy, hung back to keep company with a far more cautious Grace. As she had promised, she stayed within her brother's line of sight but felt no danger radiating from the man who now crouched near the bank of a narrow stream and allowed the cool water to run over his fingers.

Teddy did not say anything to Rosemary, only peered at her with a curious expression on his face until she finally broke the silence. "For someone with such a quick tongue, you are awfully quiet today."

He smirked. "I thought it best if I kept my opinions to myself after angering you the other night. I'd say your tongue is quicker than mine, and it's also razor sharp."

"At least you refrained from asking me if I am all right," Rosemary said with a small smile and a sigh. "That would have earned you a thorough lashing."

He raised his hand in the scout salute and said with mock seriousness, "I swear never to inquire as to your well-being ever again."

Rosemary could not help but chuckle, and the ice was broken. He had the demeanor and charisma that men of means often do, but instead of making one feel inconsequential, Teddy Barton inspired a feeling of comfortability that Rosemary guessed drew women to him like moths to a flame.

How many had burnt to cinders under his attention? That was the question of the day.

"If I might venture an opinion, you display a great deal more mettle than my sister. She always has been possessed of delicate sensibilities, and I think this whole thing has taken quite a toll. She's not acting herself," Teddy said thoughtfully. "I have to say, I don't like it. It's easy to forget how precious family is until you are faced with losing one of them."

Rosemary's throat thickened painfully, his words resonating with her. She had known how lucky she was to have Andrew in her life and had done her level best to communicate her thoughts on the matter to him as often as possible. Still, she felt that there had been more she could have done, more love she could have given. She supposed that was normal and tried to push the thought from her mind.

"I think her reaction is quite typical. Finding the deceased came as a shock to us both, and you must remember Grace believed it to be your father in that chair. I expect it will take months for her to erase those few horrific seconds from her memory."

Nor was Grace the only one who would relive the experience. Shuddering, Rosemary added, "Worse for her coming so hard on the heels of a rather unpleasant interaction with that simpering nitwit your father wants her to marry. Don't underestimate her too strongly. After all, she agreed to come with us today."

Teddy frowned while Rosemary gazed into the distance towards where Frederick's and Grace's horses had fallen even further behind Vera's. She judged she had a few more moments alone with Teddy before the rest of the group caught up.

"Are you saying Herbert Lock harmed my sister?" he asked, his tongue now the one with lethal edges.

Rosemary shook her head. "He only got as physical as grabbing her arm, but he treated her as though she was dirt under his feet." She relayed what she had heard without a single pang of guilt. Grace needed

101

someone to watch out for her, and her brother qualified as the most suitable option.

Teddy's fists had clenched into balls, and he stomped back and forth across the bank while his face turned a deep shade of red. "I should like to strangle him with my bare hands!" he roared and then stopped short when he noticed the look on Rosemary's face.

"I did not mean that," Teddy said, struggling to keep his voice calm. "Truly, I didn't." He exploded again. "I despise the sap. The mere mention of him puts me in a lather. Herbert Lock is a poor excuse for a man, and that he would treat a woman so callously proves precisely why."

Still, Rosemary did not believe she was in any danger; however, Teddy's mercurial nature wouldn't change her mother's opinion that he might be the murderer. "Why do you suppose your father thinks him a viable option, then?"

"Honestly, I have no idea." He tapped his fingers against his leg. "The bigger mystery is why Grace hesitates to make her feelings known on the matter. Father wouldn't force her to marry a man she dislikes, no matter what the reason."

"Could it have anything to do with business?" Rosemary said, leading the conversation in the direction she needed it to take.

Teddy frowned. "No, I wouldn't think so. Father isn't in business with Herbert, and I don't believe he has any intention of changing his mind on that score. We've worked diligently to ensure that Barton & Co. adheres to the letter of the law."

It was an odd thing to say, and to Rosemary indicated that, as she had already gleaned, the company hadn't always operated in an upright manner. Despite some misgivings, she said as much to Teddy.

"No," he sighed. "We weren't always on the up-and-up. That was mostly before my time, and partly due to changes in the law. However, the situation has been a right mess to clean up."

Rosemary filed the information away for further contemplation.

"As far as Grace is concerned," Teddy said, setting his jaw determinedly, "I can assure you she will not wed the deplorable Herbert Lock, as I intend to expose him for the cad he truly is. Whatever business my father has with him is over."

Now she'd gone too far, Rosemary realized and tried to rectify the oversight. "Have a care, Teddy. It's possible Herbert is a murderer, and equally possible your father was the intended target. Scaring him off at this stage of the game might send an innocent man to the gallows."

Frederick was the man Rosemary meant, but she thought Teddy might have got the wrong impression when she saw the look on his face. He started to speak, then stopped short as Frederick, Grace, and Vera approached, but his expression told Rosemary he might have regretted saying so much. Why he had been so forthcoming, she could not be sure. She hoped it meant that he had been honest with her. The two did not always mean the same thing.

Frederick appraised the pair, and Rosemary was sure he had noticed the anger that had crossed Teddy's face. She directed a smile and a nod in his direction to let him know that there was nothing to worry over.

"That was exhilarating," Grace said, her cheeks flushed a pretty pink. "I can't thank you enough for inviting us out. It certainly beats sitting around at home waiting for another argument to start, doesn't it, Teddy?" She dismounted carefully and placed a hand on her abdomen.

Her brother nodded, his eyes fixed on Grace, his expression speculative. "Indeed. Are you all right?"

"Yes, dear brother," Grace grinned. "I'm perfectly fine. Just a bit overexerted."

Vera's eyebrows scrunched together in sympathy. "I am sure the atmosphere at Barton Manor is less than jovial. Do you think, perhaps, that a small soiree is in order? At my mother's house this time. It might take the edge off. Or is it too soon?"

Rosemary caught Vera's eye and her friend winked. If there was one way to get people to open up and talk about things they normally would not say aloud, it was with whisky and gin acting as verbal lubricants. Grace's eyes lit up with excitement. "Perhaps a tad, but I doubt anyone will protest too much. Your mother hardly ever allows guests at her place. I suspect she'll have a full house."

Grace was right, Rosemary thought wryly as she climbed down from the saddle. Lorraine Blackburn could have suggested a party directly following Mr. Cuthburt's murder and half the town would still turn up.

Chapter Twenty-One

Inspector Max Whittington's mouth was drawn in a thin line when Rosemary and her entourage emerged from the stables. It surprised her to see him sitting on one of the garden benches, a cigarette in one hand. "Hello, Rose," he said evenly.

"Max. I assume you would like a private moment," she replied.

Rosemary caught Vera's arm and whispered, "Go up to the house and plan your party while I talk to Max. Perhaps we can get all of our suspects in the same room again."

"Leave it to me, my love," Vera whispered back with a wink. "I shall wave Mother as bait and none shall resist."

Teddy Barton kept his eyes on Max as Vera—and Frederick, who had overheard Rosemary's instructions—led him up the path toward the main house. The look etched on both faces told the same story; they were already aware that the other had sights set on Rosemary's affections. It had taken Teddy no longer than it had taken Max to figure out what a remarkable woman Rosemary was. Except, Max had been living with the knowledge for the best part of a decade, whereas Teddy had just become acquainted with it a few days before.

It mattered little that the woman in question was so closed off to finding another love that she chose to ignore their attention. When they were out of earshot, Rosemary took a seat and looked at Max expectantly.

"I feel it's my obligation to inform you I have come against a new line of inquiry that peripherally affects you," Max began stiffly.

Rosemary scrunched up her nose at his choice of wording and laid a hand on Max's tense arm. "I can only assume that your obligation is that of a trusted friend, and in that case, Inspector, I beg of you to dispense with the severe level of formality you are displaying," she said, just as formally but with a twinkle in her eye that begged him to comply with her request.

"I'm serious, Rosemary. Somehow, during the course of reading through all the statements made that night, I came across a discrepancy. It has to do with Mrs. Blackburn." He paused and watched as the twinkle left her eye. He was sad to see it go, especially as a result of his own words.

"Lorraine? Oh, please, you must be able to see that her attitude is no more than the affectations of an actress and a deep-seated feeling of inadequacy," Rosemary objected. The thought that Mrs. Blackburn had anything to do with Mr. Cuthburt's death had never even flitted across her subconscious, and she vehemently resisted it entering her mind now.

Max shook his head. "You know damned well I have to keep my wits about me, Rosemary. I cannot go on gut instinct alone. Of course, I find it difficult to believe she might be a killer. But I believe she's capable of having done it. Everyone is, on some level. You must know that. She has a reputation as a live wire, and she's made no secret of the fact she knows how to handle a pistol. From what I understand, she could shoot the fleas off a dog's back at fifty paces."

"Please explain how that has any significance, considering half the room was watching her every move all evening. Where does she say she was during the time of the murder?"

"In the downstairs toilet. The one at the back of the house, not the one in the entrance hall which she claims was locked when she wiggled the handle," Max explained. "One of the maids admitted to showing Mrs. Blackburn down the hall, but she immediately returned to her post and can't say where the woman went after that."

Rosemary gaped at Max. "That's still not enough evidence. You saw what Lorraine was wearing that night. She couldn't have fitted a paper clip between the dress and her skin, much less hidden a gun."

"I don't know. She could have had it in her handbag, or stashed in the coat cupboard. Regardless, I discovered a connection between her and Mr. Cuthburt. So far, all the evidence we have indicates Mr. Barton was the target. What I have found is the first clue that points to a motive for killing Cuthburt. After all, he *is* the one who's dead." Max ran a hand through his hair, frustration evident in the jerky quality of his movements.

"What evidence? You chose to warn me, so now you must give me all the information. I cannot—and *will* not—allow anything to tarnish Vera's name without solid proof. You had to have known that, or you wouldn't have come here."

Max sighed. "Yes, I believe on some level I knew that. Ernest Cuthburt and Lorraine Blackburn apparently had past connections. According to Arthur Abbot, there was no love lost between the two. Cuthburt owned the rights to a play Lorraine desperately wanted to star in—this would have been when Vera was a teenager, during the war. From what I understand, Lorraine thought it would be her big comeback to the stage, and then at the last minute, he pulled the plug."

Digesting the information quickly, Rosemary shook her head in bewilderment. "Why would a businessman like Cuthburt have anything to do with the theater?"

"He doesn't, normally. It seemed to be a departure for him. Abbot did not enjoy speaking ill of his dead friend, but eventually, I hammered out of him that he believed Mr. Cuthburt bought the rights just to spite Lorraine. It's possible their connection extends further into the past than even Mr. Abbot knows. If that is the case, well, it doesn't look good for Mrs. Blackburn."

Rosemary could recognize how difficult it was for Max to give her information that ought to have remained classified and appreciated that he had gone to the trouble, but at the moment all she could feel was frustration. Frustration and dread.

"Perhaps not. And here I thought it was only my own flesh and blood I would need to defend, and it turns out I have two people to clear from suspicion: my brother and my second mother."

Max frowned deeply. "This is still my investigation, Rosemary. However, I see no harm in you learning whatever you can from Lorraine Blackburn herself. She'll be far more candid with you than she would with me. Not, mind you, that I believe she hides much from anyone. As for Frederick, the only reason he's not in my custody now is that not a shred of physical evidence points irrefutably towards him. If anything else, however seemingly inconsequential, indicates his involvement, I will have no choice but to arrest him."

"Well, your timing is impeccable," Rosemary said, ignoring the point about Frederick, so sure of her own convictions that he couldn't possibly have had anything to do with Ernest Cuthburt's murder. "Vera has decided to throw a party at her mother's estate house this evening. It will be the perfect opportunity for sleuthing. Might I say, it feels very much like you need my help, Inspector. I do recall you implying that I'd be a hindrance to the success of this investigation."

"Yes, Rosemary. I know what I said. You can waste time poking fun at me, or you can get on with it." He couldn't keep the irritation from his voice, even though he could tell she was taking it personally. He had gone over and over the facts so many times he couldn't keep count anymore and still had no idea who had killed Ernest Cuthburt or why. Now, he was alienating the woman he admired most in the world, and there wasn't a thing he could do about it.

"Just figure out a way for me to clear your brother. I'm inclined to believe he's telling the truth, and both Teddy and Marjorie confirmed seeing him leaving Barton Manor around midnight. However, that's quite close to the time when the murder occurred, and he could have been coming from the study when he met them in the drive. Unless more compelling evidence turns up to implicate someone else, he could end up a scapegoat. Not all of my superiors are sticklers for proper procedure."

That was not what Rosemary had wanted to hear, and she recalled her brother's statement about how he had nothing to fear since he had done nothing wrong. It wouldn't be the first time Frederick had been wrong about something.

"I guess I have some work to do," Rosemary said, and after a few more minutes discussing the case, she bade the grumpy Max goodbye.

CHAPTER TWENTY-TWO

Little Nelly accosted Rosemary two steps inside the entrance to the entrance hall, and once again, she allowed herself to be caught up in the delicate smell of his soft, baby-like hair. "Why didn't you take me out on the horses, Auntie Rose?" he asked, his lower lip jutting out into an irresistible pout.

"Grown-up time, my little lamb. Before I leave to go back to London, I promise to take you riding. I am sure Wadsworth here," she pointed to her man, who had just arrived from the adjacent dining room, "would be happy to take you in my stead." She winked at Wadsworth, who blanched at the thought of riding, an activity Rosemary knew, despite his proficiency, he did not fully enjoy.

"Of course, Master Lionel," Wadsworth confirmed, refusing to meet Rosemary's gaze even though his lip quivered from holding back the urge to speak his mind. He wouldn't, as it would not be appropriate, but Rosemary guessed he would find a way to subtly get back at her later. Perhaps with another forced shopping trip that would finally result in actual money being spent. For now, all her thoughts stayed focused on helping clear her brother and Mrs. Blackburn from suspicion. Shenanigans with the staff would have to wait.

Stella and Leonard had just sat down for tea in the dining room, and Rosemary found them there with her mother, father, and Vera.

"Have Teddy and Grace gone back to Barton Manor?" she asked, sitting down and pouring a cup of tea for herself and one for Vera.

Vera nodded. "Yes. Grace claimed she had something to do this afternoon, and Teddy accompanied her back to the house to ensure she made it there safely. I believe he has become paranoid, given the circumstances."

"And where did my dear brother wander off to?" Rosemary asked.

Mr. Woolridge answered her question. "I sent him to the office to deliver some documents that needed signing. Perhaps there, he can stay out of trouble."

"I simply cannot believe the three of you!" Evelyn suddenly burst out. "Do you not listen to a single word that comes out of my mouth? I warned you about getting further involved with the Bartons, but what do you do? Set about making friends and bringing them onto our property! What on earth could you possibly be thinking?" she demanded.

Mr. Woolridge's mouth set in a thin line while the rest of the family attempted to keep their jaws from dropping on the table. "Evelyn," he scolded, "the children are involved in this matter whether we like it or not. We all are, even Stella and Leonard, who would be peripherally affected if the police determined one of us had reason to want Ernest Cuthburt dead. What do you expect Frederick to do? Just sit back and let Inspector Whittington haul him out of here in handcuffs?"

Evelyn's face paled with chagrin at her outburst, and at having been chastised by her husband in front of her entire family. Cecil reached across the table to pat her gently on the hand, a loving expression on his face. "I know you were only trying to help, my love, but our children are grown, and they can make their own decisions. Personally, I feel better knowing our Rosie is on the case. She sees things more clearly than the rest of us."

"Not everything." Ignoring Vera's comment on her lack of a love life, Rosemary felt a rush of gratitude and love for her father. It wasn't like him to lay praise on so thickly, and it bolstered her confidence in herself.

"Father is right about one thing. We can't sit back and let the police focus on Frederick. We have to look at the rest of the suspects and figure out who committed the crime before they do."

"Why don't you tell us what you know, Rose?" her father asked, sitting back in his seat and folding his hands in his lap. All eyes were on her, and so Rosemary launched into an explanation of the facts.

"First, don't invest that money with the Barton business until Teddy and his father finish taking a thorough look through the company records for anything suspect. Teddy claims Mr. Barton wants his business run legitimately. Whether those wishes are due to Mr.

Barton's genuine concern over being above board, or whether Teddy put on some pressure is another mystery."

Evelyn clicked her teeth and tongue in a tutting sound that held an edge of triumph. "Didn't I say the Bartons weren't to be trusted?"

Slanting her mother a look, Rosemary continued. "Max— Inspector Whittington—is concerned with our family's involvement, as the sum Father was planning to invest may have been exactly what they needed to legitimize the business."

Leonard, of all people, spoke up then. "Wouldn't that put your brother *out* of the running as a suspect? He has nothing to gain by killing either Barton or Cuthburt if what everyone wanted amounted to the same thing."

"As far as motive goes, yes, one would think. However, as time goes by, and there is pressure to close the case, the inspector fears the local police won't be as concerned about motives or what makes sense as they are about finding enough evidence to pinch someone. Anyone. Thankfully, Frederick is only one suspect, but unfortunately, now Vera's mother is another."

Mrs. Woolridge gasped and settled back in her chair, one hand fanning her face as though she might faint. Hers was an extreme reaction compared to Vera's; Rosemary's friend looked at her with shock-widened eyes, then set her jaw and said nothing. Then again, she didn't need to voice her outrage since Evelyn spoke the words that would have popped out of her mouth anyway. "That's preposterous! Lorraine is not a killer any more than Frederick is!"

"I know, Mother, and for now, all Max has is a tissue-paper motive and a theory. According to the inspector, Lorraine hated Ernest Cuthburt."

Rosemary explained how Cuthburt had snatched away the possibility of Lorraine appearing in the play she had her heart set on. "The police don't care if that's a thin motive; people have killed for less. That's why I need all of you to engage in a little subterfuge with me. We're going to continue on with our plans to have a party at the Blackburn estate house tonight, and we're going to find out whatever we can from the other suspects. Vera and I will talk to her mother."

"Unfortunately, anyone who had opportunity to kill Cuthburt seems to lack motive and vice versa. Except for Lorraine," she directed at Vera, "who had both if you can call losing out on the opportunity to

110

star in a play motive for murder. Max seems to think the authorities might."

"What about the rest?" her father asked. "Certainly someone else had both motive and opportunity."

"They do. Unfortunately, the other most likely suspect is Frederick, and your mother's statement that someone was locked inside the bathroom doesn't completely exonerate him. It *does*, however, prove she was in the entrance hall and could have sneaked upstairs to kill Cuthburt after the maid left her alone," Rosemary lamented.

Vera's nose crinkled as she frowned deeply. "For that matter, Grace could have done the same thing, as could have Mrs. Barton. She believes her husband has been stepping out with another woman. That gives her a motive for killing him, and she appears capable if the scorching looks she shoots every woman in every room is an indication."

The tea had gone cold, but Rosemary gulped hers down without noticing. "The trouble is proximity. People came and went from the ballroom at such short intervals, and while the study is near enough to hear the party with the windows open, it takes time to navigate the halls and stairs between them."

Running down the list of possibilities, Rosemary and Vera discussed alibis.

"Mrs. Barton claims she retreated to the kitchens to speak to the butler, but Geoffrey says it was actually Grace he spoke to during that time. Which means both of them were not in the ballroom at the opportune moment. Either of them could have gone upstairs, killed Cuthburt thinking he was Mr. Barton, and then hurried back down." Rosemary sighed. Max was right, the case was one big circle. "Unless there was a shortcut between the two rooms, nearly everyone with a motive was seen near the ballroom too close to the time of the murder."

"It's quite common to install—" Leonard began to say something, but Vera cut him off.

"Grace. It had to be Grace." She banged a fist on the table. "Grace's demeanor changed partway through the night."

"Yes, it did," Rosemary agreed. "I assumed her nerves were because of her run-in with Herbert Lock, but perhaps that was a convenient cover. What's more, she's the only one who admits to seeing the letter threatening Mr. Barton's life."

More determined, now that her mother was a suspect, to get to the bottom of the thing, Vera played devil's advocate. "Still, she'd have to be an utter piker to drag you out here, Rosie, then bump off her old man. It couldn't have been her, I don't think, after all."

"Neither do I," Rosemary agreed. "As for the rest, Teddy was in the billiard room, alibied by several other gentlemen who were also present. Marjorie pulled him away, but she could have fetched him directly after killing Cuthburt, and used him for her own alibi. Except Marjorie seems to have no motive."

The deconstruction of the crime went on for several more minutes.

"Mr. Abbot claims he saw Frederick at the bottom of the stairs in the hall, and that his actions were suspicious. Considering Freddie was so drunk he doesn't even remember collecting himself and leaving the bathroom, it's no surprise he appeared to be in distress. Abbot had excused himself to find a quiet place to administer his insulin injection, and the doctor he has on call verified that he received it. The man is a pillar of the medical community, so his statement holds water."

Vera stood and paced, picking up where Rosemary had left off. "And then there's Herbert Lock, who you and Grace left on the balcony after their altercation. He has no alibi, he's been cavorting around with Marjorie Ainsworth, and I wouldn't put anything past him."

"I think we all share that sentiment. Everyone else, including Mr. Barton, never left the ballroom, that much we know for sure since you were both there." Rosemary looked at her mother and father, who nodded in agreement. "As far as I'm concerned, Herbert as the killer makes the most sense. He was already angry. If he'd had an unpleasant conversation with Mr. Barton or Mr. Cuthburt that evening, he might have acted out of desperation in the heat of the moment. His alibi is thin, and he has a temper."

Some of the animation went out of Vera. "This is all predicated on Mr. Barton being the intended corpse. What if Cuthburt was as much a bounder as Max says? I mean, if he treated my mother so spitefully, who's to say she was the only person who ended up on the wrong side of him?"

Cuthburt appearing to have no enemies put a massive spanner in the works of the whole case.

It was a thought that stuck with Rosemary for the rest of the afternoon, no matter how hard she tried to dislodge it.

Chapter Twenty-Three

Just as Rosemary had predicted, the prominent players accepted Lorraine Blackburn's last-minute invitation and had assembled in one of the downstairs parlors. Music that was probably a touch too upbeat considering the tragedy that had recently occurred wafted from the Victrola at a volume that still allowed for conversation.

Also as expected, once she learnt of Rosemary and Vera's intent to discover Ernest Cuthburt's killer, Mrs. Blackburn had agreed to host the little get-together with a vengeance. On top of being considered a suspect, a notion Lorraine refused to take seriously, the mystery and intrigue were too tempting for a woman who thrived on drama. Now, she looked like a piece of art, coiffed to the extreme, and dressed as though she were attending an event organized by the Queen herself.

Lorraine Blackburn's slinky silk dress clung so tightly, and was of such a similar shade to her milky-white skin, that if one were to catch a glimpse out of the corner of one's eye, it might appear as if she weren't wearing anything at all. Only a delicate lace ruffle beginning at mid-thigh and skimming the floor detracted from the effect.

Rosemary shook her head as she watched the spectacle from across the room, thinking perhaps this had not been the grandest of ideas. Yes, they'd got their suspects gathered in one space, but if Mrs. Blackburn's antics distracted everyone all evening, prying information from the guests would be a chore.

Grace and her brother were cozied up to Frederick, and Rosemary got the distinct impression that, unless it turned out one of them really had murdered their dear Uncle Ernest, Frederick might have found himself a new friend or two.

Across the room, Marjorie Ainsworth perched on the edge of a gilt-trimmed armchair and sipped a gin and tonic while her beautiful, keen eyes fluctuated between attempting to catch Teddy's or

Frederick's gaze, and casting narrow glares in Herbert Lock's direction. Teddy duly ignored the woman, and Rosemary felt sorry for her until she remembered the way Marjorie had acted at the Bartons' anniversary party. She hoped her brother had sense enough to follow Teddy's lead, but he appeared intrigued by Marjorie's charms.

The most shocking additions to the party included Mr. and Mrs. Barton themselves, though it was clear that for once the obnoxious man's wife had had her way. Clearly, Mr. Barton had not wanted to attend the party, and sat sullenly in one corner with Arthur Abbot, downing expensive whisky as though it were water. Mr. Abbot's eyes widened as Mr. Barton threw another dram down his throat, but he did not caution his friend. Rosemary couldn't blame him, having seen Mr. Barton's temper firsthand.

To round off the guest list, Rosemary's own parents were in attendance. Mrs. Woolridge, as always, took great pains to make sure every other attendee knew that she was a frequent visitor to the Blackburn estate.

"You went with the cream silk wallpaper I see, Lorraine," she said loudly, just in case there was a soul left in the room who did not recognize the claim she had as the hostess's closest friend.

Mrs. Blackburn looked at Rosemary's mother blankly for a moment. "Oh, yes, you are right, Evelyn. I think it looks simply smashing in here now, don't you?"

Evelyn Woolridge would never have chosen the plum-colored sofa or paired it with the emerald-green swirl-patterned rug, but she agreed with Lorraine anyway. "It looks lovely. You're so daring when it comes to mixing patterns."

Rosemary hoped her mother would keep Mrs. Blackburn occupied with inane chatter, but also hoped she wouldn't have to listen to talk about the drapes all evening.

When Mrs. Blackburn turned off the music and stood at the front of the room, Rosemary realized that her concern regarding the woman's distracting antics had been unwarranted. After all, the actress who could so easily command a room could also use her *je ne sais quoi* to lead the conversation in precisely the direction Rosemary required.

"Thank you all for coming here tonight." Staff with trays of champagne circled the room while Lorraine stood before her guests with a solemn expression. "Won't you raise a toast to poor Ernest Cuthburt. May God rest his soul."

Brilliant, Rosemary decided as, from her vantage point, she watched faces in hopes one would reveal his or her true feelings about the deceased. None did.

The moment over, Mrs. Blackburn turned the music back to its previous volume and then ambled over to the drinks trolley and began mixing up cocktails for the guests.

Marjorie rose, and Rosemary heard her ask Lorraine where to find the toilet. "It's through that door there, and down the hall," Mrs. Blackburn answered with a smile that Marjorie reciprocated, though without the level of sincerity as the one she was given.

Recognizing the opportunity, Rosemary slipped out behind her. Marjorie headed in the wrong direction, and Rosemary helpfully pointed out the fact. "I am afraid the arrangement of rooms in this house can be rather confusing. You want to go this way."

"Thank you," Marjorie said, smiling a tight smile. She appeared drawn and upon closer inspection, her eyes were ringed with red, though it was apparent she had tried to cover the fact with an abundance of kohl.

Rosemary considered how best to proceed. Her desire to glean information was at odds with her reluctance to scare Marjorie off. "This is all rather maudlin, don't you think?" she commented wryly.

"Yes, I suppose so. Though, life does go on," Marjorie replied, turning on her heel without another word and closing the door behind her. Silently, Rosemary berated herself for thinking it would be easy to gain the trust of a woman like Marjorie with so little effort.

As Rosemary turned to head back towards the parlor, she noticed Herbert Lock, arms crossed, leaning against the doorjamb. His menacing expression set Rosemary's heart thumping a little harder in her chest.

"Quite a little sleuth, aren't you, Mrs. Lillywhite?" he spat. "Poking your nose into matters that are none of your concern."

"A man is dead, Mr. Lock, and since my brother is the one being accused of the crime, it certainly is my business. You're looking pretty good as a suspect if you ask me."

The color in his face continued to rise as he sputtered, "Why on earth would I have killed Mr. Cuthburt? We were in negotiations for a deal that would have made me a lot of money. You're obviously not as clever as you think you are."

"Unless you thought he was Mr. Barton, and that Grace had already told him she wouldn't marry you," Rosemary retorted. "Then, your plan for getting to her money would have been out of the window, and you'd have had nothing to lose." Nor would he have had anything to gain, which was the sticking point.

Herbert blanched. "This is your fault, you meddling little wench. You're the one who whispered in Grace's ear and told her not to marry me. We were just fine until you came along."

"Your mistake is in thinking Grace is the type of woman who would listen to someone else rather than her heart. However, she's the one who has decided you aren't good enough for her. Mind you, I heartily agree with her conclusion," Rosemary said, crossing her arms in a mimic of Herbert's stance, the same way a wild animal might mirror its prey.

His eyes goggled out of his head, and his arms became rigid as his hands turned to fists at his side. He wasn't nearly as formidable as he thought he was, but Rosemary still didn't wish to have to defend herself, particularly in heels.

Herbert sputtered. "Keep your nose out of our business, or you might live to regret it," he threatened, coming toward her with a look of sheer rage on his face.

Marjorie exited the loo and stopped short, taking in the scene before her. "Herbert, leave her alone. You always aim above your station; it is truly ridiculous. Return to the party. Now."

Had he been a cartoon character, steam would have poured out of Herbert's ears as he looked back and forth between Rosemary and Marjorie. Swallowing heavily, he let out a frustrated grunt before turning around and walking back in the other direction.

"Thank you," Rosemary said quietly.

"You probably would have come out on top. That man is an utter arse," Marjorie replied.

"I hope Mr. Barton realizes that before he ties Grace to him for life."

Marjorie rolled her eyes. "Don't believe every word Grace Barton says. That one is not quite as innocent as she would like people to believe. Whatever happens to her will be well earned."

"What do you mean?" Rosemary pressed.

"Honestly, Herbert was right about one thing. You would do better to stay out of matters that do not concern you," Marjorie retorted, striding back into the parlor with a toss of her golden hair.

Chapter Twenty-Four

Rosemary made a beeline for her friends, her mouth set in a grim line. "That was a complete waste of time. All I discovered was that Marjorie has some ill feelings towards Grace. She seems to feel the same way about me, though what I've done to irritate her I couldn't say."

Vera closed her eyes for a moment. Sighing, she shook her head from side to side. "Rosie, dear, you can't be serious. For someone with your deductive skills to turn into such a dumb Dora is annoying beyond the telling of it at times."

"So nice to see what you really think of me." Rosemary was miffed.

Enunciating clearly and drawing the words out slowly, Vera explained. "She doesn't like you because Teddy does." Vera had every confidence that her friend would ferret out who killed Ernest Cuthburt, but she worried that when it came to her own personal life, Rosemary would turn a blind eye to the most obvious of clues.

Clamping her mouth shut, Rosemary flushed and refused to comment. Vera tended to view things from her own perspective. In her presence, most men turned to drooling dolts, and so she thought the tendency a common trait of the species instead of a normal reaction to her own magnetism. Rosemary—in her personal opinion—never had, and would never inspire enough interest in a man to spark jealousy among the female population. Ergo, Marjorie had another reason for her attitude, and Vera was deluded. That was the only explanation that made sense.

She was considering the possible reasons when her mother appeared at her side. "Lorraine has offered the ladies a tour of the gallery. Would you like to come along?"

Vera and Rosemary exchanged wry looks. The gallery, as she called it, was a room full of paintings for which Lorraine had posed. She took great delight in shocking her guests as some of the paintings were nudes.

"Thank you, but no. I've seen the gallery many times before."

In the end, only Mrs. Barton, Marjorie, and Evelyn took the tour, leaving the men and Grace behind.

Directly after the chattering group had left the room, Rosemary and Vera busied themselves mixing up a complicated cocktail. Teddy and Grace, the latter's face still slightly pink from Vera whispering the truth of the gallery in her ear, joined the pair near the drinks trolley to offer opinions as to whether gin or vodka made the best martinis. Rosemary split her attention between them and the rest of the people left in the room, straining to overhear the conversation between her father and Mr. Barton.

When he noticed Rosemary's uncharacteristic silence, Frederick said, "What's the matter, Rosie? Have you gone into a trance, or are you merely cogitating the results of a bout of sleuthing?"

"Hush now, Freddie. Were you aware your voice goes up in direct proportion to the number of drinks you've had?"

"Edgar, Arthur," Cecil Woolridge said, taking a seat near the pair. "I think I've finally decided that perhaps membership of the club might suit me after all," he said, following the plan he and Rosemary had discussed before the start of the party.

Mr. Barton, having already become so inebriated that Rosemary could smell his breath from right across the room, boomed with laughter. "I knew we'd convince you eventually, Cecil. You must buy a set of clubs, of course. I can get you a deal there, old cove." Mr. Barton appeared far more excited about the idea than it deserved him to be, and Mr. Abbot simply nodded in agreement with whatever his partner said. Rosemary imagined, given Mr. Barton's personality, things worked that way most of the time.

"Does this mean you're considering our offer?" he asked Mr. Woolridge.

Rosemary's father nodded. "I am considering it, Edgar. Of course, I'll need to consult Frederick first. The young guard, don't you know. Must bring them along in the ways of the business world."

"I think it would be wise to advise waiting to make any changes to our business structure until after this murder investigation has been closed," Mr. Abbot cut in, his eyes serious.

Cecil Barton shrugged off his concerns. "We're on the up-and-up, Arthur. Ernest made sure of that before he died. He combed through all the records with a fine-tooth, and there's no reason in the world why we shouldn't move forward as planned. This deal will make us all a lot of money, and then we can retire to the golf course full-time."

Mr. Woolridge raised an eyebrow, ignoring the comment about retiring entirely. "Why would Ernest have needed to comb through the records?"

"Oh, poor Ernest had convinced himself one of our deals wasn't strictly on the level. I believe he had become quite paranoid about protecting his reputation. Fortunately, he never did find anything, and it all added up."

Herbert Lock, who had made his way closer to the group, snorted. "I wouldn't necessarily go that far, Edgar. After all, the man is dead. Perhaps things weren't as cut and dried as all that."

Mr. Abbot looked at Herbert with surprise in his eyes. "You shouldn't speak ill of the dead, boy. It's not proper."

"Neither is murder, old chap. And neither are cooked books," Herbert retorted. Mr. Abbot didn't reply immediately, but it appeared he might have had a response at the ready. As he opened his mouth, a commotion outside the door caught everyone's attention.

When it opened, they could hear the shrill voice of Mrs. Barton, who was screaming at the top of her lungs. "You're a no-good floozy, and if you think you'll worm your way into this family, you had better think again! Stay away from my son, and stay away from my husband, or I'll make you sorry you were ever born!"

"That's rich, coming from someone who would allow her daughter to marry a cad like Herbert Lock. Not so worried about marring your good family name now, are you?" Marjorie answered, holding herself with far more composure than Mrs. Barton was.

Herbert's expression was one of shock and anger. "How dare you drag me into whatever this is, Marjorie? What have I ever done to you to deserve this kind of attack?"

Marjorie whirled around to shoot daggers at Herbert with a single glance. "You know exactly what you've done, Herbert. I'm sure Grace will attest to the fact you've tried to strong-arm her, just like you tried to strong-arm Rosemary in the hall earlier tonight."

"He did what?" Frederick piped up, and by this time the entire room was in an uproar. "Did he put his hands on you, Rosemary?" her brother demanded.

"Calm down, Freddie, he didn't touch me." Rosemary debated whether honesty was the best policy in this situation, not wanting to start another world war right there in Lorraine Blackburn's parlor, but ultimately decided on the truth. "Though, I have to give Marjorie credit for interrupting our conversation. I can't say for sure whether he would have resorted to physical violence, but it wouldn't have surprised me in the least."

Frederick turned his fury and his fist in Herbert Lock's direction. "It's time for you to leave, or I will see to it you exit with fewer limbs than you arrived with."

Being half sozzled on Lorraine Blackburn's best booze, Frederick's aim went wide, and the blow merely glanced off Herbert's jaw. Herbert returned fire with a short-armed jab that swelled Frederick's eye.

Oddly, the one-eyed gaze improved Frederick's aim because with the next punch, Herbert's nose gave a satisfying crunch and, just as Teddy made to step in and defend his sister's honor, the fight was over.

Blood welling between the fingers clutching his nose, Herbert looked from Frederick to Theodore and decided he was outclassed in the fight. "Fine," Herbert said, "I'll go. But this isn't over."

"I think it's time to wrap this party up," Mrs. Blackburn said.

"I agree." Marjorie stalked out of the parlor without so much as a goodbye, and the slamming of the front door echoed behind her.

For once, Edgar Barton was too stunned to bluster, and with his wife leading the way, he and Arthur Abbot followed her out.

"I'm devastated, Lorraine. You must accept my sincerest apologies for my son's behavior. Fighting like a hooligan in your beautiful home." Red-faced and profuse, Evelyn threw herself on Lorraine's mercy while the woman in question merely grinned delightedly.

"Don't trouble yourself, Mrs. Woolridge," Vera assured. "Mother absolutely thrives on drama. She'll mark this down as her most successful soiree to date." Without seeming to be rude, she ushered the Woolridges towards the door.

"Come along, Frederick." By his tone, it appeared Vera's assurance had not mollified Cecil Woolridge.

"I think I'll walk home. I need some air," Frederick said. "You will come straight back to the house with Wadsworth." It wasn't a question, but Rosemary nodded in agreement, anyway.

Perhaps it had been a bad idea to get everyone back in the same room.

"That was quite a spectacle," Rosemary said as she slumped into a chair and kicked off her shoes. She took a long swig from her cocktail, which by now was room-temperature, and sighed.

Vera settled onto one of the other settees and mimicked her friend. "You have to admit, the expression on Mrs. Barton's face was priceless when she burst through the doors screaming at Marjorie. I realize Mr. Barton is loaded and all, but it's obvious Marjorie has her heart set on Teddy. Something tells me she's put the final nail in that coffin, though."

Rosemary raised an eyebrow at Vera. "Mentioning coffins probably isn't very tasteful."

"I think tasteful has gone out of the window after tonight," Vera replied wryly. "Though I do feel sorry for poor Mr. Cuthburt. It seems the world would be a better place if it had been Mr. Barton who had died, after all."

"It wasn't as though Ernest Cuthburt was a pillar of virtue, Vera. He probably deserved what he got," Mrs. Blackburn retorted, matter-of-fact.

Rosemary's ears perked, and her eyes widened slightly. "Mother!" Vera exclaimed. "It would do you well not to say such things, considering Inspector Whittington already thinks you might have had a vendetta against the dead man. What could you possibly be thinking, saying something like that?"

"Vera, dear, you worry far more than a carefree young girl such as yourself ought," Mrs. Blackburn chided. "Do you see Inspector Whittington around? Is he skulking outside the window, listening in on our conversation? I think not. Besides, I would say the same thing to him if he asked. I have absolutely nothing to hide."

Groaning under her breath, Rosemary attempted to pry information from Vera's mother, a task none too difficult what with Lorraine's loose lips and the exorbitant number of cocktails the woman had consumed.

"Was the play he stole from you really worth him dying over?" Rosemary asked. The idea that Mrs. Blackburn could be that vindictive didn't line up with Rosemary's opinion of her.

"The play?" Lorraine asked, surprised. "Of course not. Don't misunderstand, it made me want to rip him to shreds—verbally, mind you, not literally."

"Well what then, Mother?" Vera implored.

Mrs. Blackburn looked between the two as though they were daft. "Why, Ernest Cuthburt was a war profiteer. He managed to make a killing from the blood of our sons. Didn't you know that?"

CHAPTER TWENTY-FIVE

Rosemary woke the next morning with a feeling of dread in the pit of her stomach. Without Vera's comforting presence by her side, nightmares had intruded on her subconscious, and images of each of her loved ones being sent to the gallows kept her from getting a wink of decent sleep. Not that she blamed Vera for wanting to stay behind with Mrs. Blackburn. Eventually, Rosemary would have to return to London and go back to her cold, empty bed anyway. She sighed and readied herself for the day. A good strong cup of tea would wake her up, she hoped, as she headed downstairs for breakfast.

Frederick was already seated, looking a little worse for wear. "Did you sleep at all?" she asked him with a raised eyebrow.

"No, not really. And it doesn't appear that you did, either, dear sister. Nightmares?" he asked, already knowing the answer.

She nodded while loading her plate with buttered toast, steaming eggs, and perfectly cooked sausages. The rest of the family trickled in, and soon they were all seated around the dining-room table. An unusual hush had settled over the group, though it was clear the events of the previous evening and the murder of Ernest Cuthburt were still fresh on everyone's mind.

"I don't know how you're able to withstand this pressure, Freddie, and still seem like your jolly old self," Stella's husband said, shaking his head in astonishment. Rosemary, both irritated by her brother's ability and impressed with it at the same time, couldn't help but agree.

He flashed them both a toothy grin, though Rosemary thought she might have caught a niggle of doubt under the surface.

"The evidence they have isn't enough to put me away. Several people were milling about the house, so why I would be top of the list is beyond me. I couldn't have fired a gun with any precision given the state I was in, regardless. They'll move on and find the real killer, eventually."

"Proximity may play less of a factor than the inspector believes," Leonard stated. "I wouldn't be at all surprised to find there was a secret passage." His observation set off a discussion about where such a passage might be concealed and who might have had access.

A lively debate ensued until Rosemary asked the maid to fetch her sketchbook and attempted to draw the house from memory. All discussion of dimensions was cut short and promptly forgotten when the doorbell rang several times in quick succession.

Moments later, the butler ushered Inspector Whittington through the dining-room door, and Rosemary felt a profound sense of déjà vu. Max's expression was similar to the one he had worn the last time he had interrupted breakfast at Woolridge House, except this time it held even more with regret and foreboding.

"Frederick Woolridge, I'm here to place you under arrest," Max said, looking at Rosemary and then Mr. and Mrs. Woolridge with an apology in his eyes. "For the murders of Ernest Cuthburt and Herbert Lock."

A stunned silence followed Max's statement, and then the room erupted into chaos.

"Oh my heavens," Mrs. Woolridge breathed, and then fainted into the arms of Wadsworth, who appeared surprised to have found himself in such a position. Rosemary was thankful for his quick reflexes but didn't have time to worry about her mother's latest dramatic reaction to bad news.

"Herbert Lock is dead?" she asked, stunned.

Mr. Woolridge's voice held more emotion than Rosemary had ever heard it possess before, "You've made a mistake!"

"I sincerely hope so, but yes, Herbert Lock was found in his room at the inn. The innkeeper found him and called us early this morning. It seems he was shot with the same gun that killed Mr. Cuthburt. Because we have verified Mrs. Blackburn's whereabouts for the time of Cuthburt's murder, she's no longer a suspect. Frederick's altercation with Lock last night pushed him to the top of the list."

The inspector turned to Frederick. "I'm afraid I will have to take you in, now. I'll delay the inquest as long as possible, but unless some new evidence surfaces soon..."

Rosemary had never seen Max at a loss for words, and it made her blood run cold. She shivered and wrapped her arms around herself to keep from breaking down.

"The chief inspector has returned, and it's his belief that your brother murdered Mr. Cuthburt over some bad business. I'm beginning to understand why Andrew went private, Rose. The man won't listen to reason. Unfortunately, it's been confirmed that Frederick and Herbert had a row last night and that it turned physical. It was a gunshot wound to the head that killed him, but I can't ignore that the two of them came to fisticuffs mere hours before his death. Furthermore, it seems Frederick walked home from Mrs. Blackburn's, which gives him opportunity."

Turning to Frederick, he said, "If there is any proof you arrived home before the time this murder occurred, out with it now. I believe it might be your only hope."

Rosemary's face went white as a sheet. "We'll have to consult the staff, but the house was quiet when I arrived home at approximately half past midnight. I saw a light under Frederick's door and heard him moving around in there on my way to bed. What was the time of death?"

"Between half past ten and half past eleven. I'm told the party broke up at around half past nine, which means the deceased had just enough time to get back to the inn, clean himself up, and get ready to sleep. His pyjamas were laid out on the bed, but he had yet to don it when the killer arrived."

"Which means in all likelihood, my brother doesn't have a solid alibi. Did anyone see you arrive home, Freddie?" she asked, looking around at everyone in the room.

Frederick shook his head, for once not looking so self-assured, and it was clear from the expressions on the rest of their family's faces that nobody else could honestly say they were positive of the time he had arrived at Woolridge House.

Max reluctantly led Frederick to the front door, only stopping long enough for Mrs. Woolridge to wrap her arms around her son and sob uncontrollably. Her husband had to force her to let Frederick go, and Rosemary could tell from the look on Max's face he deeply regretted having to be the one to cause her family more pain. The look in his eyes said it all.

126

"I promise all of you I'll do whatever I can. Rosemary, I fear much of the responsibility will rest on your shoulders now. Do whatever you need to do, but keep your family and your friends around you. Stay safe, and contact me if you find out anything useful. Mr. Woolridge, Mrs. Woolridge." He nodded to them on his way out, his head hung low.

Once the car containing Frederick had pulled out of the drive, Mrs. Woolridge lost her composure entirely and had to be escorted to her room and administered a sedative. Rosemary wished she could take one herself and simply wake up discovering that this whole ordeal had been one bad dream. Instead, she summoned Vera and went to work.

Chapter Twenty-Six

"What makes you think she will talk to us, Rosie?" Vera asked as Wadsworth pulled the car up in front of a tiny cottage on one of the village side streets.

Rosemary swallowed hard and said, "Marjorie didn't appear to have much respect for Herbert Lock, but she had some sort of relationship with him. What I'm counting on is that she's now even more desperate than she was before. We both know Teddy can't stand her; her hopes of getting her money back died with Herbert, and now the only other eligible bachelor in her sights is in jail. If it comes down to it, I believe she might, in her current condition, respond to a well-worded threat."

Vera appraised her friend and found that although fear for her brother's freedom and reputation roiled beneath the surface, Rosemary was now operating on the sheer force of determination. "You really don't understand just how amazing you are, Rosie dear. Let's put the screws on her; it would make us both feel better."

It would have made Rosemary feel better, but when Marjorie opened the front door, she lost all will to brutalize the woman. The usual sparkle was gone from her eyes, and her face was puffy from crying. She held a handkerchief in one hand, her hair stood on end, and she was wearing a robe over bare feet. "Whatever do you want?" she asked, but there was no bite to the words.

Rosemary changed tacks and answered with a gentle, "May we come in, please? I realize we hardly know one another, and I'm aware that you don't care for me particularly, but we have a common goal."

"There's nothing you can do to help me, so why would I help you?"

"Correct me if I am mistaken, but I thought you enjoyed Frederick's company. Have you no heart? You know he's not Herbert's killer."

Vera could hold back no longer. "This is a ghastly business. Never mind, Rosie. It seems Marjorie hasn't the wit to realize that bodies are dropping like flies, and hers might be the next one to fall. Leave her to her misery and let her fend for herself." Taking her friend's arm, she tried to pull Rosemary away.

"Wait." Marjorie opened the door wide enough to allow her unwanted guests entry. With a look of triumph, Vera sailed inside to watch Marjorie crumple onto a comfortable, if threadbare chair. Seating herself on the settee opposite, Rosemary appraised the sparse surroundings of the cottage, noting a few framed photographs of Marjorie and two people she assumed were her mother and father.

"Do you live here alone?" she asked, unable to help herself.

Resigned, Marjorie said, "Yes. If you must know, my aunt left me this cottage when she passed away. But I didn't let you in here so you could judge me and ask a dozen questions about my personal life. My parents are dead, I have no other family to speak of anymore, and I've had to learn how to take care of myself. It's left me with little patience, and you're wearing it thin, so why don't we just keep to the topic at hand?"

Her words had been meant to put Rosemary in her place, but she couldn't help feeling a bit of grudging respect for Marjorie Ainsworth all the same. "All right then, why don't you start by telling us who you think killed Mr. Cuthburt and whether you think the same person murdered Herbert."

"I believe it's obvious that the deaths are connected, but I don't know who would stand to gain anything by killing Ernest Cuthburt. Of course, I didn't know the man well, but all the interactions I'd had with him were pleasant enough. He seemed like a good egg to me."

"Then I assume you're unaware of his war profiteering." Rosemary let the information slip out and watched Marjorie's eyes widen with surprise.

"No, I wasn't." She shook her head. "But it doesn't make the whole thing any clearer."

"We agree," Vera replied this time. "The point is, he could have had enemies. Mr. Barton did as well, and my guess is that he was the intended victim. I believe you might have a better idea of why he might have been targeted. I saw you arguing with him on the balcony."

Marjorie lifted one eyebrow but otherwise didn't react. Rosemary had to admit, she was hard to shake. "You think I'm the one who tried to bump him off? All I wanted was my money back. Herbert thought getting close to Grace would help convince the Bartons to invest in his business venture. Perhaps if he'd done his research more thoroughly, they would have. Barton told him he needed to go back to square one and work out a more appealing proposal. Herbert switched tacks, and when I made it clear I was never going to be his wife, set his sights on marrying Grace for the money. I believe he planned to cut me out entirely. I had hoped that Teddy would take a shine to me and negate the whole situation, but he made it clear he wasn't interested." It appeared a difficult thing for Marjorie to admit, and her face bunched into a scowl. "So, I was left with no other option than to blackmail Mr. Barton."

"Are you saying you're the one who sent him the threatening letter?" Rosemary asked with bated breath.

Puzzled, Marjorie shook her head. "No, I don't know anything about any letter. I did hear Mrs. Barton accuse her husband of being involved with a woman of loose morals, but she had no idea with whom. I simply communicated to Mr. Barton that I'd give her a name if he didn't help me out of the jam Herbert had got me into. He was furious, but I thought perhaps I'd hit my mark. Then Mr. Cuthburt was murdered, and I had no choice but to bide my time. After Mrs. Barton's outburst last night, it's all out in the open, and I'm out of options. I'll lose this house, and everything else I care about."

Rosemary felt a tingling of pity for the woman, but it was mixed with disgust when she asked, "What about my brother? Was he just another mark?"

Marjorie's chin wobbled, and for the first time, she appeared genuinely contrite. "No, he's not. In fact, I told Teddy the night of the party that I'd back off. I felt guilty about the blackmail attempt as soon as I'd made it, and I wanted to wash my hands of the whole thing. I know you probably don't believe me, but that's the truth."

"I can't say I'd be thrilled with the idea of you and Frederick, given the circumstances," Rosemary said with an edge to her voice, "but I do know my brother is intrigued by your...charms.

Unfortunately, it won't matter if he's convicted on two counts of murder."

"What can I do? I don't know who killed either of them," Marjorie said, her eyes sliding away from Rosemary's.

"But you have a suspicion, don't you?" Rosemary prodded.

Marjorie sighed. "I know Grace threatened Herbert. She told him he'd be sorry if he continued to pursue her, and I know that her father still considered Herbert a viable suitor. He'd played his cards well enough to convince Mr. Barton that he was merely a novice businessman with potential. I doubt Grace took too well to her protests falling on deaf ears."

Vera's eye caught Rosemary's, and she hung her head. "I'd hoped it wouldn't come down to that, but you might be right." She couldn't deny Grace Barton had the strongest motive. "We'll take it from here, but if you want even a slim chance of getting closer to my brother, you'll cooperate with us if it becomes necessary."

"You have my word."

CHAPTER TWENTY-SEVEN

Rosemary instructed Wadsworth to pull up outside Mrs. Shropshire's and practically jumped out of the car before it came to a complete stop. "Madam, please, allow me to assist you," he said as he bounded out of the driver's seat.

"I'm fine, Wadsworth, don't worry about me. We won't be a minute." She tossed the last over her shoulder as she pulled open the tearoom door.

Mrs. Shropshire stood behind the counter with one of the employees, patiently explaining how to tally the cash register money at the start of a shift. She looked up when Rosemary and Vera burst through the door and toddled over to them with curiosity in her eyes.

"What do you girls need?" she asked without preamble.

When Rosemary asked to use the telephone, the old woman pointed her towards an alcove adjacent to the kitchen. Rosemary thanked her and dialed while Vera explained what they were up to.

"We've got to get hold of Grace Barton immediately and see if we can find out what she's been hiding. Rosemary wants her either cleared from suspicion or pinned to the wall. We know she has a secret, and the secret may be that she's the murderer!"

Mrs. Shropshire's eyebrows lifted. "Grace? I thought you had decided the poor girl was innocent."

"We had," Vera said, "but new information has come to light, and now there's another body."

"I know. It's all anyone can talk about. Word is poor Mr. Lock was shot with the same gun as Mr. Cuthburt. Half the villagers are hiding in their homes lest they end up dead."

"That's ridiculous," Rosemary replied, rounding the corner from the telephone room, "neither of these crimes was random. It's not as though there's a crazed axe murderer on the loose."

"Oh, they're enjoying it, really." She grinned. "Nothing exciting ever happens around here. You two be careful, you hear. You're putting yourselves in danger. I expect to hear from you by the end of the day, else I'll worry. You understand me?" Mrs. Shropshire's tone brooked no refusal, so Rosemary and Vera promised to ring her as soon as they could then insisted they must be on their way.

They piled back into the car just in time for Wadsworth to hear the tail end of Rosemary and Vera's conversation. "Who exactly are we following?" he asked, his tone dry as desert sand.

"Grace Barton," Rosemary said in a tone that mirrored the one Mrs. Shropshire had just used. "That snooty butler of theirs informed me she had business in London and would leave within half an hour. He declined to disturb Grace and insinuated that I shouldn't be bothering her. Thank you, Wadsworth, for, well, for being you."

"My pleasure, madam."

They were in luck when Grace's car pulled onto the street and headed in the direction of the village. Her pale face was visible through the cracked rear window, and she wore an eager expression that smacked of deceit to the pair of sleuths who trailed her. Wadsworth angled the car out of the chapel lane where it had been hidden behind a bank of shrubbery and followed several car lengths behind.

"It appears Wadsworth has done this type of thing before," Vera commented absently.

"I wouldn't be at all surprised if that were true," Rosemary said, thankful the partition between the front and back seats was up so he couldn't hear their conversation. "Andrew asked him to drive occasionally, and I always wondered why when we had a full-time driver on call."

Vera peered at Rosemary, suddenly more focused than she had been previously. Days had passed since Rosemary had last mentioned her late husband, and for the first time, her voice had lost some of the bitterness and anger.

"Does investigating make you feel closer to him?" Vera asked, hoping it was the right thing to do and then deciding she didn't care if it wasn't. They were long past the point where propriety dictated their actions towards one another, and she knew Rosemary would ask tough questions if their roles were reversed.

133

"It does, yes," Rosemary said, her eyes taking on a dreamy, faraway quality. "It's as though he's guiding me, somehow. The pain is less when I'm able to think of him as he was when he was alive instead of focusing on the fact he's gone. I wonder if he'd be proud of me, or angry that I'm taking a risk."

"I believe he would be proud of you, Rosie," Vera said. "In fact, I'm sure of it. I also believe he would want you to move on, eventually, and be happy with someone else."

"You'll have to forgive me, Miss Pot, for finding humor in your advice. While I might be the kettle, we are both of the same dark hue."

Lionel had been gone far longer than Andrew, and Vera showed no sign of settling down.

"We are cut of a different cloth, Rosie my love. I find pleasure in the gay life of parties and harmless flirting. I've had my share of men. Andrew would want you happy," Vera repeated.

Rosemary's eyes welled with tears. "I know that he would, but that doesn't mean I'm ready to do so. You must understand."

"I do, my love. I do. When this is all over, you and I will take a long holiday. We'll sit by the sea and breathe in the salty air, and let go of our demons once and for all."

They followed Grace all the way to London, and into a section of town that wasn't considered fashionable by any means, but where the streets were clear of debris and several businesses had set up shop. Wadsworth lowered the partition as Grace's car pulled to a stop on the side of the road. She exited, pulled her coat over her shoulders, and looked furtively around as she crossed the street and entered an establishment.

Rosemary practically pulled Vera from the vehicle and glanced up at the sign above the door where Grace had disappeared. "It's a chemist's shop," she stated with a raised eyebrow.

"Perhaps she's planning on taking another stab at murdering her father," Vera mused. "This time with a little addition to his nightly decanter of whisky." Her cheeks turned pink as she realized what she'd just said. "That wasn't nice. I suppose I'd rather it turn out to be Grace than have Frederick hang for the crime. Still, I shouldn't have said that."

"Don't worry, I won't tell anyone you had a moment of weakness," Rosemary promised while she threw caution to the wind and pressed her face close to the glass to look inside the shop.

It was empty as far as Rosemary could tell, except for Grace, who stood at the counter talking furtively with the man behind it. Something in the way she held herself, leaning towards him, and her expression told Rosemary this wasn't a man Grace had just met. It was a man with whom she had a relationship, and the pieces began to fall into place as Rosemary recalled some of the things Grace had said.

The comment about Grace having no trouble finding a husband floated through Rosemary's mind.

"I'm uncertain whether this helps her case or worsens it, but I believe we have discovered the reason Grace was so against being forced to marry Herbert Lock. Or, more accurately, one reason, aside from the fact that Herbert was an utter cad." Rosemary crossed her arms while Vera took a peek.

Grace reached across the counter and touched the chemist's hand. He looked down at where her fingers lay against his skin, then back up with a regretful expression. The two spoke for another few moments, and when Grace exited the shop, her eyes were ringed with red. It was a look Rosemary had become accustomed to seeing on the woman, and Teddy's comment about his sister being fragile came flooding back.

"Well, that was illuminating," Vera said as she and Rosemary ducked back into the car to keep out of Grace's sight. "What do you think, Rosie? Is she conspiring to kill her father, or has she gone and got herself in the family way?"

Ignoring the choked sound made by Wadsworth, Rosemary allowed, "Either scenario might accomplish the same end." Guiltily, because the image brought her some measure of pleasure, she pictured the apoplectic face of Mr. Barton should he learn his unwed daughter had a pea in the pod.

"Remember how she acted when we took the horses out?" Vera reminded Rosemary. "Extraordinarily cautious, even though it was clear she's a more than proficient rider. I thought it was odd at the time." Speculation on the subject continued as they made their way back towards Pardington when Wadsworth's dry voice cut through the talk.

"I believe you shall get your chance to talk with Miss Grace on the subject." He brought the car to a halt along the verge. There, in the road, stood Grace's driver and the woman herself leaned against the boot of the car.

That Grace had worked herself up over something was evident in the look on her face.

Rosemary threw open the door without waiting for Wadsworth, only to have it nearly torn off when another car whizzed by.

She took her time and checked the road before she tried again, and once she had alighted from the car, stood beside it. Grace strode over to Rosemary and Vera, her face contorted into a look of fury. "What are you two doing here? Why did you follow me?" There was more color in her face than Rosemary had seen for days.

"Because you left us no choice," Vera answered acidly. "You're in love with that man, aren't you?"

Grace stared at Vera as if she'd gone mad. "Yes. Yes, I am in love with him. How does that affect you?" she asked, seemingly baffled by why Vera was so angry.

"Because, Grace," Rosemary answered, "it gives you a motive for attempting to murder your father and Herbert Lock. Those murders are now being pinned on my brother, Frederick."

Goggling, Grace fanned her face with her hand. "When you said you believed I had nothing to do with this, you were lying. I can't say I'm surprised. It isn't as though either of you has ever attempted to be my friend before. I ought to have known you weren't really my friends now."

She reached for the car door handle.

"Grace, wait," Rosemary called, "please. For Frederick." Her voice was pleading. Against her better judgment, Grace turned around.

"I," she enunciated carefully, "murdered no one. Particularly not Herbert. Father might be full of bluster, but there are ways around him if one is patient."

Head tilted, Rosemary assessed Grace's face and posture for signs of prevarication, and finding none, had to relent. "I'm sorry, Grace, for not believing you. One does, however, have to put family before friendship, and my brother is being locked away for a crime he didn't commit. You must understand my position. I can't afford to dismiss anyone out of hand. How would you feel if it were Teddy?"

136

Grace didn't have a chance to answer because Vera, who had listened to Rosemary's apology incredulously, was the next to speak. "Rosie, you can't be serious!" she exclaimed. "We can't keep confronting suspects and then just believing them when they say they didn't do it. She could be lying."

"I'm not lying," Grace snapped.

"Do you honestly believe Grace is guilty of murder?" Rosemary spoke to Vera as though the subject of the conversation weren't standing three meters away.

Sighing, Vera's shoulders drooped and she admitted, "No, I suppose I don't."

"Then let us stop wasting time chasing after her, shall we?" Rosemary suggested.

Grace threw her hands in the air and rolled her eyes when Vera finally acquiesced the point. With little else to say and a light drizzle beginning to fall, all parties proceeded to Pardington.

Wadsworth turned towards Woolridge House while Grace's car continued on down the road in the direction of Barton Manor. Anna must have been watching out of the window because as soon as they pulled up she emerged from the house with a large umbrella, ushering Rosemary and Vera inside before they took a soaking in what was now much more than just a drizzle.

Chapter Twenty-Eight

The arrival back at Woolridge House saw Rosemary feeling defeated and at a loss. Her head was swimming, and all she wanted to do was take a nice, long bath. Vera declared she could use a bit of fresh, albeit exceedingly damp air, and elected to pull on a pair of wellies and take a walk out to visit the horses while Rosemary retired to her bedroom.

"Anna, please make the water as hot as possible," she said, rubbing the kink that had become lodged in her neck and shoulders.

"Yes, madam. Is there anything else I can get for you?"

With a shake of her head, Rosemary declined. "No, no, I'll just find my slippers and close my eyes for a moment." She remembered having kicked them underneath the bed and bent down to search. Her eyes lit upon a sheaf of papers, the sketches she had begun the night of the Bartons' anniversary party.

Retrieving them, she moved to the desk and noticed the sketch she'd been making when she'd realized Frederick hadn't returned from the party. Instinct rose up to set her blood thrumming in her veins. There was something here, she simply knew it.

Rosemary leafed through the drawings, memories of the evening returning once more to swim vividly behind her eyes. There was the desk, strewn with papers and detritus, behind which Mr. Cuthburt had met his end; there was the ballroom where Rosemary had captured the allure of Mrs. Blackburn in shades of charcoal, as well as the look of envy on Mrs. Barton's face; and the vision of Grace standing stiffly next to her father and mother.

At the bottom of the pile was a sketch that made Rosemary's hands shake with excitement and hope. Quickly, she snatched up the drawing she'd made at Leonard's behest and compared the two.

"Oh my heavens," Rosemary breathed, rousing Anna's attention away from her task of returning a pile of dresses to their hangers. "I know who the murderer is."

Anna blinked a couple of times and dropped the garment she had been holding.

"Drain the bath and go and find Vera, please. Tell everyone to gather in the parlor. I'll be right down."

The maid nodded and complied, leaving Rosemary alone for a moment. She was grateful for the reprieve and the opportunity to collect her thoughts. Glancing down at the paper in her hand, Rosemary shook her head and chided herself. She might have been able to spare Herbert Lock's life, and Frederick's misery, had she come to the realization sooner.

It's impossible to start at the beginning and skip straight to the end. Andrew's words bubbled up from her memory. *It's in the middle where we discover the truth.* Rosemary stood up, collected herself, and said a silent thank you to her late husband for having been a man who could comfort her even from beyond the grave.

"It's Arthur Abbot. He's the murderer," Rosemary explained to her family once they were all gathered in the parlor. "Look at this." She showed them all the sketch of Mr. Cuthburt emerging from the coat cupboard beneath the stairs in Barton Manor's entrance hall. "I knew something wasn't quite right about that little room, and I've finally figured out what. It's the end of a secret passage that leads upstairs."

Vera's face cleared as she caught up with Rosemary's supposition. The others, save Leonard, who was grinning like the cat who ate the canary, appeared somewhat confused.

"Don't you see? He popped out, killed Ernest Cuthburt, and then took the passage back down. He wasn't counting on Frederick seeing him, but even so, he wasn't close enough to the stairs or any other known exit, and therefore aroused no suspicion," Rosemary explained. "I'm right, I can feel it. Despite the incongruous nature of her personality, I've never truly believed Grace was responsible."

Rosemary ignored Vera's smirk since she had, indeed, thought Grace a possible killer at one point.

"All Grace wanted was to get out from under her father's thumb and marry her chemist, a man of whom she thought Mr. Barton would never approve. There are other ways to accomplish that without resorting to murder, and I'm positive she doesn't have the stomach for it. We've already counted out Mr. Barton, Teddy, Marjorie, and of course poor Herbert Lock. Mrs. Barton never left the ballroom all night and was alibied by the staff for the time of the second murder. All the pieces fit together nicely."

Her father drummed his fingers on the table beside his chair and slipped a sliver of doubt into Rosemary's conclusion. "What about Abbot's alibi? That physician fellow stated that Arthur was with him, in one of the sitting rooms off the ballroom, from half past eleven to nearly midnight."

Rosemary faltered, her mind searching for an explanation, and wondering how a man who couldn't remember what he ate for breakfast could suddenly recall the specific details of Mr. Abbot's alibi. "The simplest explanation is usually the correct one. The physician is lying. I'll just have to prove it."

"Maybe not." The admission came from the most unlikely of mouths: that of Mrs. Woolridge. "We only need him to confess. Isn't that how they always do it in books? Set a trap, get him to talk. Don't the criminals always want to tell their story? Then we can let the inspector handle the rest."

Stella's eyes nearly popped out of her head, but she kept her mouth firmly closed. "Wipe that look of incredulity off your face, daughter," Evelyn said anyway. "I want this case closed, and my son returned so we can all go back to our normal lives. If it means a little game of entrapment, well, that's exactly what we'll do."

Everyone present nodded their heads in agreement. "For Frederick," they agreed and set about making a plan.

"What about the Bartons? Do you suppose they'll go along with it?" Rosemary posed the question that, if not answered in the affirmative, would throw a spanner in her idea.

Her father stood, determined. "Never you mind about the Bartons. I'll take care of them. Give me a few moments." He strode out of the room and returned a short time later with a smile upon his face.

"I told Edgar we'd discovered who the murderer is and that if he didn't cooperate with my requests, he wouldn't get another penny from

140

Woolridge & Sons. He confirmed that he has been out hunting ever since he heard the news of Herbert's death, and he hasn't spoken to anyone outside his family all day."

The pieces fell into place as several calls were made. Mrs. Woolridge left to ring Mrs. Blackburn and then, when she had finished, left the door open for Vera. Once Marjorie Ainsworth was instructed to find herself at Barton Manor later in the evening, it was Rosemary's turn to make a call.

"I need to talk with Inspector Whittington, please." Rosemary's mouth formed a thin line as she listened to Max's landlady's reply. "Do you happen to know when he's due back?" Another pause and she let out a sigh. "Can you please tell him Rosemary Lillywhite needs to discuss a matter of some urgency? Yes, he will know how to get in touch with me. Yes, I will try his office. Thank you."

Rosemary depressed the receiver to disconnect and then immediately placed another call, but still could not reach Max. "Drat," she spat, before returning to the parlor. She hoped her message would reach him in time, but reassured herself that if it came down to the wire, the local police would have to do in his place. Then, she summoned Anna for the final preparations.

"We don't have time to wait for a messenger, and since Arthur Abbot has not been to Woolridge House since we arrived, that means you're the only one he won't recognize," Rosemary told her maid. "I'm counting on you to deliver this to him." She handed the shaking Anna a sealed envelope. "Wadsworth will drive you. I trust he can keep from being seen unless it's necessary. There will be a special bonus in it for you."

Anna didn't appear to relish the thought of delivering a message to a murderer, but she trusted her mistress and decided the possibility of a new dress or perhaps a pair of shoes was worth the risk. Once she had departed, it was time to wash and ready for an evening of subterfuge.

"What about us?" Stella asked before anyone else could exit the parlor, indicating herself and Leonard. "We don't want to miss out on all the excitement yet again."

Mrs. Woolridge raised an eyebrow at her daughter. "You have a child to look after, dear. It's best if you stay behind where it's safe."

For a moment Rosemary thought her sister would do as she always did and submit to Evelyn's demands without argument. However, it seemed Stella had reached her breaking point. "Mother, if you want another grandchild out of me, I'd suggest you have second thoughts. We're coming, and that's final."

Rosemary wished she could have the expression on her mother's face captured on canvas and hung on the dining-room wall for all to enjoy. She and Vera chuckled over it all the way back to Rosemary's rooms, where they quickly dressed and readied themselves.

Back downstairs, Stella examined her son while the nanny stood nearby waiting to take Nelly up for a bath and bedtime. "Whatever did you get into, little one?"

"I was playing out in the barn. I was a pig. The pony thought it was funny. He licked my whole face," Nelly explained, causing Stella to wrinkle her nose.

"Well, I'm glad I didn't kiss your cheeks, then," she said, but Nelly had already turned his attention to Rosemary.

"Tomorrow you'll take me on the horses, won't you, Auntie?" he asked, his eyes so full of hope Rosemary couldn't have denied him even if she'd wanted to.

"Of course, darling," she replied, and then nearly keeled over when Nelly launched himself into her arms. Rosemary hugged him close, sent him upstairs, and then realized her mistake. "I'm covered in mud. Drat. I'll have to change. Why don't the rest of you go on ahead? I'll come along behind with Wadsworth. Vera as well, if she doesn't mind."

"Where you go, I go, remember?"

The rest piled into Mr. and Mrs. Woolridge's car and headed down the lane while Rosemary changed her clothes for a second time. When she met Vera at the bottom of the stairs, she was slightly winded and eager to get on with the events of the evening.

Rosemary exited the front door, avoiding a strip of darkness created by the shadow of Woolridge House that splayed across the driveway, and shivered in the cold night air. She rejected the idea of going back inside for a coat and climbed into the backseat of her car with Vera at her heels. "Wadsworth, get us to Barton Manor as fast as you can," she said, raising her voice so he could hear her through the closed partition.

He didn't answer, but pressed the accelerator and made his way down the lane. Rosemary wrung her fingers as she thought about what was ahead of her and was so distracted she didn't notice when the car took a right-hand turn rather than continue up the hill where Barton Manor loomed.

"Rose, why are we headed in this direction?" Vera asked, puzzled.

"Wadsworth, you're going the wrong way." She pushed the window that separated the front seat from the back and gasped when she realized it wasn't her butler at the wheel, but Arthur Abbot. He had a gun in his hand, and he glared at her in the rearview mirror.

"Neither of you will make it to Barton Manor tonight. Because tonight, you're going to die"

Chapter Twenty-Nine

Rosemary froze, wishing she could open the door and jump out, but unwilling to leave Vera in the hands of a madman and knowing she probably wouldn't be fast enough to dodge a bullet, anyway. What she wished even harder was that she'd been able to alert Max to her plan. Now, with her own life in jeopardy, she regretted having acted with such haste. That she'd been right about Arthur Abbot provided little comfort.

He spun into the lane leading to the chapel and revved the engine before coming to a stop at the entrance of the cemetery that butted up against the southernmost edge of Barton Manor's grounds. Before Rosemary or Vera could do anything other than lock panicked eyes, he had yanked open the rear door and ordered them out of the vehicle.

"Move. Now." His voice was far calmer than his demeanor, his shaking hands speaking volumes about his mental state.

"Mr. Abbot, Arthur, please. You don't have to do this." Struggling to keep her breathing under control, Rosemary had little hope of help arriving in time, if ever, to save them. It was one thing to take self-defense training, quite another to be thrust into the position of needing to use it. Half the lessons had gone out of her head and the other half she couldn't use because Abbot had a gun.

Arthur met Rosemary's plea with a sneer. "Don't I? You keep poking your nose into everything. I thought framing your brother would keep you busy. Women are supposed to do what they're told and not try to think for themselves. Not clever enough, though. I sprang your little trap."

"Why…" Vera took offense but bit off the scathing retort before making matters worse. "How did you figure it out?"

That's right, Vera, keep him talking, Rosemary thought to herself, taking the moment of reprieve when Abbot shifted his gaze towards her friend to search for anything—a weapon, or even a large stone—that might get them out of this predicament.

Mrs. Woolridge had been right; Mr. Abbot wanted to talk. He wanted his story told, and since he meant to kill them anyhow, it didn't matter what he let slip.

"I knew you would be trouble as soon as I realized you were chummy with that Inspector Whittington. Did some checking up on you, didn't I?"

If only something would distract his attention, Rosemary thought she might be able to save Vera. Her own life mattered little compared to that of the precious one in danger now because of her.

Meanwhile, Abbot's diatribe continued. "You'd be surprised by what I found. I know your husband used to be a private eye, and I know you set that party at the Blackburn estate as a trap. I overheard that idiot brother of yours when you thought my attention was on Edgar. It wasn't." The more he worked himself up, the shakier became the hand holding the gun.

Nothing in her training had prepared Rosemary for dealing with a man like Arthur. Hard-nosed attackers, yes. Nervous men with pistols and nothing to lose, no.

Breathe and wait for an opening. That's what Andrew would do.

"I didn't miss Herbert's little slip-up either. He knew about the second set of books. He could have told the police about it, and I'd have been up on charges within a fortnight. But instead, I killed him. And then I followed you. All the way to London." Caught up in his tale, Abbot's eyes turned misty, and the grip on the gun loosened slightly.

Rosemary noticed. She prodded him. "When we were following Grace?"

"Yes. You were so concerned with not being spotted by Miss Barton you didn't notice you were being followed. Almost solved my little problem on the way back, but you were too quick for me. Another second, and I'd have hit you with the car. Slipped up there, right enough. Women playing at being detectives, I ask you."

"What about you?" Vera might have been acting tough, but her fingers trembled. "You think you're so clever, but you will not get away with this. Before you kill us, don't you want to know how we saw the problem with your alibi for Mr. Cuthburt's murder?"

That was brilliant Rosemary thought, *stall until we figure a way out of this.*

Abbot continued as if he hadn't heard Vera's question. "I waited for you, you know, and when you got home, I saw that maid bring you an umbrella—you must pay her rather well with your dead husband's money—and so I recognized her when she appeared later with a note supposedly written by Mr. Barton. You managed to get his signature just right, I'll give you that."

"But why?" Rosemary still didn't know the answer to that question, and if she couldn't figure out a way to disarm the man, she'd go to her grave never understanding. The thought bothered her almost as much as dying did. "Why did you kill Mr. Cuthburt? You were friends and business associates."

"Business associates, yes. Friends, never. That man was responsible for killing my wife. He was a war profiteer, you know, would have done anything to make a few quid. It's not all about commodities and the black market. Cuthburt preferred to make his money in the back alleys of London. He owned a theater there, under an alias, of course, selling spirits at a ridiculous markup for those who could still afford to imbibe."

Rosemary hoped Abbot would get caught up in the story and forget about the gun. While she listened, she watched closely.

"That was on the face of it," Abbot said. "In the back, he provided a place for his real customers—the crooks and the cons who managed the organized crime syndicates of London. Isabella worked there as a cocktail waitress. We didn't have a lot of money. We were only starting out, but I begged her to give it up. She refused, saying she wanted more for us, a better life. One night after her shift, she disappeared. They found her body, bloodied and bruised, in an alley not far from the theater. Of course, Cuthburt never accepted responsibility, and I've spent these last years making a name for myself, getting close to Cuthburt so that when the time came, I could ruin him."

"Ruin him? You've done more than ruin him, Arthur. The man is dead, and so is another young man who had his whole life ahead of him. Surely your wife was avenged after the first death."

"I didn't intend to kill Cuthburt!" Abbot boomed, becoming more agitated and less careful with the weapon he held in his hand. "I wanted him broke, behind bars, with his reputation in the privy. I wanted him to suffer. Instead, he went quickly, unlike my poor Isabella."

Keenly agitated, Abbot appeared ready to cry but shook his head to clear the notion, and continued to rant. "I didn't mean to kill him. But he—he practically goaded me into it. I watched him sneak up to Edgar's study, so I followed him. He was rooting around in the desk, and when I confronted him, he said he had finally figured out what I'd been up to."

"Which was what, exactly?"

"Why, framing him for something that might actually stick this time. Oh, Cuthbert had vowed to clean up his act. He'd only agreed to work for Edgar if he promised to legitimize Barton & Co. once and for all. So, I had to help him along. Let's just say, if the police had found *my* copy of the books, Ernest would have been ruined. If Herbert Lock had just minded his own business, he'd still be alive."

Rosemary shivered, sensing Arthur Abbot's patience was nearing its conclusion and wished she had gone back inside for her coat after all.

"Now, which one of you would like to go first?" Abbot said, waving the gun between Rosemary and Vera as though playing a game of Eeny meeny miny mo. "I choose...you." He pointed the gun at Vera. "So your friend can watch you die knowing she could have spared you if she'd simply minded her own business."

In a final effort to stall, Vera said, "Don't you want to know how we solved the mystery?"

The man paused, his curiosity and hubris getting the best of him. "How?"

"Your mistake was in attempting to frame Frederick," Vera explained. "You told the police you were near the entrance hall when you were supposed to be with your physician instead."

"Max Whittington will put it together," Rosemary said. "You can kill us, but he will solve the case and come after you." Her faith in the inspector was unfailing.

"Not if I take care of him first. Who else knows? Your father? The butler? Well, he won't be talking."

"What have you done to Wadsworth?"

"Little tap on the head. He's probably not dead. Yet."

Red rage roared up inside Rosemary like a thundercloud, and she felt adrenaline pulse through her veins as she shoved Vera unceremoniously to the side, ducked, spun, and aimed the pointed end of her heel at Abbot's weapon hand. A shot rang out, and for a long moment, Rosemary felt her heart breaking into a million pieces.

Then, almost in slow motion, Abbot's eyes widened in shock as blood seeped from the wound in his chest, spreading to turn his shirt from bright white to scarlet red. He stumbled back and then fell to the ground and stilled.

"Rosemary!" She heard Max's voice from the other side of the car and squinted in the blinding glow of the headlights. Relief flooded her heart as she scrambled to gather Vera into her arms. Max circled to where Abbot lay and checked his pulse to make sure he was indeed dead.

"Did you have to ruin my new frock?" Vera complained. "There's a run in my stocking."

There was blood on her knee as well, but the injury was minor.

His voice ragged with emotion, Max returned to where Rosemary cradled Vera. Whatever else he might have wanted to say, all he could manage was, "Rosemary. I … are you hurt?"

"A bruise or two. Nothing worse."

"How did you know where to find us?" Rosemary asked. "Did your housekeeper tell you I called?"

"No, but I'd only just walked into the station when the third of a series of irate phone calls from a woman named Mrs. Shropshire came through. She claimed you were supposed to get in touch with her, and that she had been unable to get through to Woolridge House. I went there, and the maid said you were at Barton Manor, but when I saw a light near the church, my instincts brought me here."

Rosemary helped Vera to stand and limp to the car. "Are we free to go? It's Wadsworth, you see. I need to get home and see if Mr. Abbot has killed him."

"Go. I'll see to things here and come along to take down your statement as soon as I can. We will talk about your utter lack of concern for your own safety at a later date."

Threat or promise, Rosemary could not tell and decided it didn't matter. What she did know was that if she ever needed him, Max would be there. The thought provided comfort and also provoked a feeling

Rosemary wasn't capable of dealing with quite yet. Eventually, she would have to, but for now, she allowed herself to be escorted back to Woolridge House and her warm, safe bed.

Chapter Thirty

Yet another large breakfast was taking place at Woolridge House, this time with the additions of both Vera, who had, as promised, refused to leave Rosemary's sight, and Mrs. Blackburn, who had stayed in one of the guest rooms.

Wadsworth had survived his encounter with Mr. Abbot, and despite the bandage he wore, insisted he was fit for duty. One look at his pale face and Mrs. Woolridge had banished him to the kitchen, ordering Anna to fetch him a plate.

When her solicitous attitude toward someone who was, even vicariously, under her employ drew incredulous stares from her family, Evelyn huffed and stuck her nose in the air.

In fact, she held that very posture when Rosemary's steps could be heard on the stairs. Concerned looks passed between those assembled, but nobody said a word when she walked into the dining room wearing a dress the color of summer grass. Instead, they all stared while she marched over to the buffet table and began to load up a plate.

Frederick jumped up and beat Vera and Stella to Rosemary's side. "Let me get that for you," he said gently.

"Frederick Gerald Woolridge, I'm perfectly capable of filling my own plate." She slapped his hand away with a grin. "And I do not want your filthy fingers anywhere near my bacon."

"Everyone," Frederick said wryly, "I believe she's just fine." He went back to the table but kept his eye trained on his sister. He had, of course, known what she was made of, but he had not spent the previous night reveling in his freedom but worrying about what the encounter with Arthur Abbot might have done to Rosemary. "We know the whole story, and there's really no need to talk any more about it."

"Wait!" Rosemary exclaimed. "We still don't know who wrote that threatening letter to Mr. Barton."

"Oh yes, we do." Evelyn Woolridge preened. "You just missed it, dear. It turns out, it was Mrs. Barton all along. She wanted to scare him into acting like a faithful husband. Apparently, it isn't just Mr. Barton she watches like a hawk, because she figured out that Grace had found the letter and burnt it before you ever arrived at the manor. Also, both Mr. and Mrs. Barton have decided that perhaps a nice, boring chemist would be the perfect match for Grace after all. They've agreed to let her accept her young man's proposal, providing he makes a good impression at dinner next week."

"I guess we've tied up all the loose ends," Rosemary said, relief evident in her tone. "Except one. Come on, Nelly dear. I promised you a ride on the horses, and a ride you're going to get."

Rosemary tiptoed into the downstairs office of Lillywhite Investigations late the next night, after she'd returned to London and when the staff had gone to bed. The house was quiet as she closed the door softly behind her and walked across the soft carpet to stare at Andrew's desk chair. She sat down on it and pulled her robe closer around herself.

She glanced at the empty space above the door where the loud ticking clock used to hang and decided she didn't much care for the silence it left behind after all.

Pushing the harrowing events she'd recently experienced out of her mind, Rosemary tried to bring herself back to the place she'd been before Grace Barton had shown up on her doorstep. Finding it more difficult to imagine the space as an art studio than she had that day, she pulled open the top drawer to search for something to draw with.

I know I left a pad and paper in here somewhere, Rosemary thought to herself. When the drawer got caught halfway open, she reached her hand inside and realized there was something stuck there. Jiggling the drawer and the object, she wrenched it free and found herself staring at a rectangular box that looked like it might have been intended as a gift.

She wasn't sure she could bear the thought of opening something that Andrew had bought her before he died, but she couldn't stop her hand from lifting the lid and pulling back the tissue wrapping.

151

When she saw what was in the box, Rosemary let out a laugh that would have summoned Wadsworth in seconds had he been awake and listening. It was a replica of the sign that sat on Andrew's desk, the one that said "Andrew Lillywhite, Private Investigator," except it was Rosemary's name carved into the wood.

There was no card, and Rosemary found that she didn't care. She needn't have been explained the significance of the gift, because it was evident by the very nature of it what her husband's intention had been.

No, she thought, *I'm not ready to close down Lillywhite Investigations. Not just yet.*

-The End-

Don't miss the next book in the Mrs. Lillywhite Investigates series: *The Murder Next Door.*

Made in the USA
Las Vegas, NV
16 December 2021